ALSO BY

CORI

DISEASE OF AMBITION

TITLELESS

MEDIOCRE ENDINGS

GLUTTON FOR DESPAIR

ABNORMAL POETRY

PRICE OF THE TRINITY

CHARLES PRICE

SPOILED RICE

SURVIVING NEW AMERICA

ILLUSION/DELUSION

TOXIC LITERATURE

BIRCH

ICONIC MISERY

PARKED IN THE FLOWERBED

The characters and scenarios in this book are fictional. Any similarities with real life people, places, or things are coincidental and exaggerated. None of this actually happened.

# Green Skin

# Patrick Attaway

## Chapter 1

Wilson comes out of the stall and nods at me as he leans in to wash his hands. The only time we run into each other anymore is in the bathroom, and he's starting to grow colder each time I make a joke about him being handsome or riding off into the sunset with each other while riding a llama.

"How's that wife of yours?" Wilson asks.

"Can't keep her hands off me," I say.

"Who could with that thick head of hair?"

He gestures at his shaved head, though there's an outline of his hairline just above his ears. Instead, Wilson keeps a beard of some sort throughout the year. Sometimes he shaves it so he looks like Sam Eagle from the Muppets.

"You got a few more years before you get this," He says.

"I think mine is thinning in the back," I rub my crown.

"RIP," He laughs. "Ain't that the worst?"

The last time I got a haircut, the lady pulled her hand mirror out to ask me if the back looked okay. That's when I saw the pale circle in the back. I'm only twenty-seven, and my father isn't bald. My maternal grandfather didn't go bald. However, some gene skipped a couple generations and decided I should lose my hair as if I'm trying to hide the fact that I'm going bald. It couldn't be from the front like Jack Nicholson. No, it had to be like those guys in their forties on E Harmony trying to find their soul mate after a second divorce.

Before I sit back down at my cubicle, Kendra pulls out one of her earbuds and slaps her palm on my desk.

"Hey Wayne," She says, "When you submitted my claims for NCP last week, did you staple the W9 form to each of them?"

"I don't even remember yesterday," I say.

"Well, you know if they get denied, I'm going to have you do them over."

"Why would I do your work again when you're here now?"

"Why wouldn't you do it right the first time?"

"How about I not do it at all the next time you're out?"

Lisa, our team lead, leans over from her chair to look at us as if we're fighting about whether or not grasshoppers and crickets are the same thing instead of working more claims.

"Sit down, Wayne," Lisa says. "Kendra, I saw him print out the W9s and cover letters last week."

Kendra turns her Post Malone back on and returns to ignoring the world's existence. Similarly, I pull on my headphones to keep listening to Marc Maron's interview with Evan Peters. Some people actually work the full eight hours with just the ambient sounds of the industrial sized printers and people like Kendra and me bitching at each other.

Since 2017, I work medical claims and appeals for EHR Interactive. For about fourteen bucks an hour, I can really put my bachelor's degree to good use in a field I didn't even know existed until I applied for the job. I graduated in 2015 thinking I'd get some job experience for a year while taking a break from school, and eventually apply for a grad program. That plan took me all the way to 2019, and I'm still not annoyed enough with my career to go back to school.

Admittedly, I like having a job I don't take home after I clock out. Whatever I want to do with my remaining five hours before bedtime is my charcuterie board. That usually involves sitting in a drive-thru with my wife, Lynn, for thirty minutes, watching an old sitcom on Hulu while we eat, lying on my couch with my Nintendo Switch controller keeping my thumbs taut, and burning a layer of skin off in the shower before going to sleep with *The Office* on.

I know that this is life for most people. They work a job, go home to do nothing, and eventually retire or die of cancer before they're seventy. Sometimes they take a few days off to get sunburned in the Gulf of Mexico. However, I'm twenty-seven with a wife who is twenty-four, and she's beginning to think we're too young to be so old. I think that's a direct quote she stole from a show on HBO.

Management wants us to work fifty claims a day. I usually get fifty done before eleven. Kendra gets thirty done by four. Lisa says I'm the second most productive claims analyst in the entire company, which obviously amounts to a bucket of piss since my pay only got increased by fifty cents this year.

The department director, Ron, told our managers who instructed our team leads that there's enough turnover that there won't be any layoffs in 2020. Considering some people aren't even making thirty-thousand a year yet, I'm not surprised people are leaving. Many of us oversee millions of dollars coming through insurance companies to the doctors, yet we're making less than fifteen dollars an hour. Sure, the CEO tells us that without our work, none of this company's prospects and accomplishments would be possible. I'm sure Sam Walton's ghost says the same thing to Walmart cashiers.

The sky is orange by the time I leave the building and my Ford Escort is hot enough to kill a baby or cook a Hot Pocket. My apartment is five minutes away, but I wish I could use traffic as an excuse to come home late. Instead, Lynn comments that I'm late if I don't show up by 5:40. Well, she used to.

She also used to make dinner so we could eat by the time I got home. Most evenings, she's lying face down on the bed with her phone providing the only light in our room.

"Hey," I say.

Lifting a leg in the air, Lynn lets me know she's still alive and breathes hard out of her English Pea nostrils.

"Taco Bell?" I ask.

"Ugh," Lynn says.

"Why don't you tell me what you don't want, and we can work from there?"

"No to Taco Bell," She says. "I'm fine with Subway, Jimmy Johns, Krystal, and pizza."

Last time I ate Krystal burgers, I prayed to God that if he relieved me of my pain as I shit my stomach lining out that I'd never eat there again. I'm sure He's used to broken promises, though.

"What kind of pizza do you want?" I ask.

"I don't know."

This is likely why I'm going bald. How can she say No to pepperoni, though? I wouldn't marry someone who would order supreme. Sausage and peppers on a pizza reminds me of bird doodie on a black Porsche.

As I'm evacuating all the water and Coke Zero I drank today, Lynn walks up to the bathroom door and stares at me. This usually means she wants something. That something could be a hug or financing a new car.

"I think we need a new bulb," She says. "Your skin looks yellow."

"Racist," I say.

"You pee too much."

Lynn is snoring on the couch before I finish the last slice of pizza. If I turn the TV off, the silence will wake her. Every few minutes, her phone lights up from a notification. She's friends with people I've never met. They're not from our alma mater or her last job. Somehow, Lynn built a network from home.

After my shower, I lie down on our bed naked with some moisture still on my back. Veins pump hard throughout me. I cannot cure Lynn's depression or find her a job she won't want to quit. When we met in school, she was working to pay her way because she was estranged from her parents. Since she was old enough to work, Lynn held down a job.

There hasn't been a catastrophic event. Neither of us cheated on each other, and I don't abuse her. We don't get into shouting matches. After quitting her job at the library, Lynn stopped talking as much. She wouldn't laugh at stuff we watched on TV. The weekend trips to Target, Dillards, and At Home stopped. No question I asked her got a real answer. It's rare she'll even want me to touch her.

Kendra wheels over to my cubicle and holds her notepad as if she's taking notes on everything she perceives I fuck up on. I stop my podcast and look at her.

"Have you been outside a lot?" She asks.

"What'd you mean?"

"Are you feeling alright?"

"Sure."

"Your skin just looks a little darker or something. Did you try dying your hair last night or something? There's a little green on your hairline."

"No," I say.

"Lisa," Kendra snaps her fingers. "Lisa studied cosmetology. She'll know."

"What, child?" Lisa doesn't even look up from her desk.

"Look at Wayne and tell me he hasn't tried coloring his hair."

Lisa squints before getting up and coming over to inspect me. All I wanted to do was download these medical records for an appeal to United Healthcare. At least four times a day, I have to submit them through Optum.

"Wayne, what did you try to do to your hair?" Lisa bends over. "You too young to be doing all that, child."

"I didn't do anything but shampoo it last night," I say.

"Then maybe you need to scrub a little harder, because it's looking green up at the top of your forehead."

I put my headphones back on and they both laugh as if scrutinizing me at work is warranted. Of course, five minutes later I'm looking at myself in the bathroom trying to figure out why my hairline is suddenly green at the edges. Maybe it's been slowly changing like the thinning hair in the back I didn't notice before? I've never heard of stress causing someone to go green, though.

My skin does look less pale too. The color is a little unnatural. Whenever I'm in the sun, my skin turns red for a few days before returning to paper stock white. What if my liver is giving up on me? Neither of my parents drink, so I never took interest in alcohol either. In fact, my father is a minister. He'd probably tell me to pray it away.

By the time Kendra and Lisa are gone, I'm Googling why my skin might be changing suddenly. Am I jaundiced like a baby? Maybe it's cancer. Everything on the web eventually leads you to thinking you have cancer. I don't know if hepatitis is any better.

My primary care provider is able to see me the following Monday. By now, the yellowing of my skin is more pronounced, so if I'm experiencing some sort of organ failure, I'm at a moderate decline. Dr. Till first saw me in his office when I was a teenager and had a curious eye infection that caused long strings of puss to come out. Now, he should be retired, but he's still seeing patients on a daily basis.

"You don't have a temperature, your eyes look fine, I don't sense anything off about your blood pressure or pulse, so we'll need to draw blood," Dr. Till says. "I can do it here, or you can go across the street to the lab later this week."

"Just get it over with, I guess," I say.

A nurse comes into the exam room with a needle and two vials to take samples, and Dr. Till licks the end of his thumb trying to see what the green around my hairline is about. No, it won't come off. In fact, the scalp under my dark hair appears entirely green.

When the nurse tries inserting the needle, my skin doesn't break. I don't even feel a little pinch. She looks at the doctor, who tilts his head.

"Let me try," He wheels over.

Dr. Till holds my wrist while pressing the needle's end into a plump vein, but it's not entering my body. When he pulls the needle away, the little mark has a green hue.

"Butterfly," He snaps his fingers.

"I'll be right back," The nurse says.

"Has this ever happened before?" I ask.

"No," He shakes his head. "If we can't draw blood through your arm, we can't test your liver functionality. I can order an MRI, but I'm afraid your insurance won't give us authorization. I might have to admit you to the ER."

"Then I'll get a bill for three thousand dollars," I say. "Plus, the ER doctors are out of network with Cigna."

"You claims analysts know your stuff."

The butterfly needle doesn't do the job either. I can hear Dr. Till on the phone with Cigna's pre-authorization department, and he tries explaining my situation. I imagine if he documents that my skin is changing colors and they can't draw blood, he can fax my records after submitting the CMS-1500 form. Personally, I would print out the form and staple the records in a certified envelope.

"Well Wayne," Dr. Till comes back, "I'm going to have you in and out of here in about fifteen minutes. If you'll follow Teresa, she'll have you change into a gown and we'll take a look."

"Are you submitting the imagery to another provider?" I ask.

"Yes," He nods.

"They'll need pre-auth too. Otherwise, they'll get a denial."

"Oh, it should be fine."

"26 modifier codes end up getting denied a lot more than you think."

I'm not going to get any information for another week. Lynn meets me in the carport in her t-shirt, underwear, and no shoes on. For a moment when I hug her, I breath in her scent and remember when she wasn't miserable. The early days in school when she was a freshman living in a dorm room and spending nights in my apartment worrying her RA that she'd been kidnapped. We had sex back then. Skipped a few classes just to stay in bed together. Sometimes I don't bother waking her up from the couch to come to bed at night.

With the hall lights off and shadows leaning on my skin, I finally see that the yellow Lynn saw was just a light shade of green. I'm not going to tell her about the needles or MRI. However, whatever is changing in me is unavoidable. She's going to see my decline firsthand. With her state of mind, Lynn won't be any kind of caretaker either.

"Do you want me to cook something?" Lynn asks.

"We don't have any meat thawed," I say.

"What do you want for dinner, then?" She asks.

"Burger King?"

"Eww," She pulls away from me. "No Burger King, no Wendys, no Taco Bell, no pizza, and no KFC."

"I never want KFC."

"I'm just saying."

"Okay, what about McDonalds?"

"Fine," She says. "But you're driving."

## Chapter 2

As I'm folding claims into envelopes, my Microsoft Teams chirps with a notification from the HR lady. I saw her at the last all hands meeting and thought she was attractive in an understated way in that she was obviously old enough to be my mother yet had the physique of someone you'd want to cuddle with if stranded in a cabin during an ice storm. Somehow I doubt she's calling me up to her office for a trip to the mountains, especially given my appearance makes most corpses look sexy.

Our office building only has three floors, but I take the elevator because my blood pressure won't tolerate the stairs. The third floor is for the software engineers, security offices, and executives. We lowly analysts don't venture up here often. My colleagues refer to the bottom floor as the basement as if we're cretins kept away from sunlight, but there are windows on an entire side of the floor looking out on the scenic parking lot.

Miranda's office is smaller than my manager's on the bottom floor, and she doesn't have any windows nearby. However, her smile could absolutely fool me that she's actually happy to see me.

"Hey Wayne," She curtly nods. "You can have a seat. Really, you're not in trouble or anything, but I did want to reach out because of some concerns from your colleagues."

"I know I have a right to confidentiality," I say, "But I did go to my PCP last week and I'm fine. Well, I'm not suffering from a contagious disease, if that's what you're worried about."

"Right. We do have to make sure that you're not introducing something that could hurt others in the work place, and my other concern is that your work might be facilitating stress that's influencing your condition."

Most of my work stress comes from Kendra nagging me and Lisa enabling her, and our manager, Tracey, being unqualified for her position while reminding everyone that she's in charge. Two weeks ago, she found a claim I printed for Blue Cross Blue Shield and asked Lisa to scold me for not submitting it electronically. What she didn't know, because she hasn't worked a claim in four years, is that BCBS also accepts claims for third party plans, and they automatically reject all electronic claims missing their alpha prefix. Admittedly, I also find it annoying that all of her emails read like they're written by a third grader.

"Are you about to ask me for a doctor's note or to sign something?" I ask.

"Our official position is concern for you and your colleagues' wellbeing."

If we're ever trapped in a cabin together, she just lost out on me taking care of her needs before my own. Unlike those men you hear about in internet memes, I know how to find the clit, will put my tongue in places they won't, and can be a real sweetheart in our post-coital haze.

"You could always let me work from home," I say.

"Let's not get impractical. You're welcome to continue working in the office if you assure me that you're not housing an illness that will affect employees in your immediate surroundings."

"I'm sure everyone will give me a wide birth when I walk past them."

For now, Miranda tells me to move my belongings and equipment to one of the rows away from everyone. I'm actually happy about this because I can avoid Kendra. She doesn't even take her headphones off to ask me why I'm taking my monitors out of my cubicle. No one around appears to even give a shit. They'll all gawk when someone gets fired, but me going to another row seems to be exactly what they want.

I suppose it says something about my productivity and efficiency as an analyst that I'm not getting outright fired. My site pays this company close to six-hundred-thousand a year for software and claims follow up. Originally, I worked a little pulmonary site in Virginia that was a one-doc-shop. By the end of my first year, I had another pulmonary site and a urology one in Texas, and a doctor in Illinois that only reviewed test results for other providers. That's how I know about claims with 26 modifiers getting denied without prior authorization. There's not a lot you can do in those situations, so I tried hard balling Aetna's denial by billing the patient.

Healthcare providers bill patients whenever there are certain denials. If there's an issue with their policy such as a lapse in coverage or coordination of benefits adjustment code, then the patient gets their full balance in the mail until they rectify the issue. COB denials only require the patient to call their insurance and update who is their primary and secondary insurance providers. If they're smart, they'll ask their insurance to go ahead and reprocess their claims. Sometimes a rep from BCBS or UHC will call me asking to resubmit a claim when a patient updates their COB, but that's a trap. People who work in the claims departments of insurance companies don't directly interact with their customers, so the customer care reps are the ones calling me instead of their own claims department to placate the patient. Resubmitting a claim without corrections and a frequency level 7 on the CMS-1500 results in a duplicate denial, so I always tell the reps that they need to reprocess on their end or the patient will continue to receive invoices and be sent to collections.

However, there's another reason we bill patients. If we submit medical records, a reconsideration, or even have a hard time dealing with insurance over the phone, sending the patient a bill is a way to bluff the greedy bastards not paying their claims. The patient will either contact our call center or their insurance first. If they call us, we tell the patient to contact their insurance because they're refusing to pay their claims. Having an angry customer can do wonders for getting claims paid.

But there's some gray legality involved. Worst case scenario, Center for Medicare Services will get involved and audit a provider. This can result in hefty fees. Some providers get put out of business. However, it's not terribly common and the issue is usually resolved within a few weeks.

I billed an Aetna patient for a missing pre-auth denial. My rationale is that we tried getting the claim paid through an appeal, and I explained to Aetna that this provider doesn't see the patients in person at all. He merely interpreted their test results. Without him, their PCP couldn't correctly diagnose and treat the patient. Aetna didn't care. Beside the fact that Aetna has a bad habit of misplacing appeals we send via fax and certified mail, they're not as big as BCBS and UHC, but they sure as hell act like it.

Around 8:30 one morning, I got a call from an American Aetna rep who had his own office. Most insurance companies outsource their customer care reps to India. An American rep means they're taking things a little more seriously. As such, they act like the provider is going to roll over for them. I am not one of those people.

"Hey there, Wayne," He said, "I'm calling because a patient reached out to us regarding getting billed for services they received in August from Dr. Sellick, but number one, they claim they never saw him, and number two, I see that we already sent you a denial for an appeal, so I was hoping to get that cleared up."

"Okay," I said.

Instead of continuing the conversation, I like the silence marinate for a couple minutes. They think you're going to immediately comply with their request. Insurance companies act like they pay your claims, so you should play ball the way they want. No, a doctor will gladly bill a patient thousands of dollars, exceed their two allotted appeals, and even get their lawyer involved before they write off entire accounts. I mean, it usually doesn't get to that point. One side caves eventually. I've had to write off many claims, but that's after fighting for a provider to the extent that my resources allow.

"So, are you writing off the balance?" He asked.

"Oh, no," I said. "We've already informed Aetna that this provider doesn't see any patients at all. He interprets their labs, hence the 26 modifiers. He can't get prior auth for any of his patients because he doesn't even get the results until the lab is done processing them a week later."

"Yes, I understand that, Wayne, but you can't bill a patient for these services."

"Are you going to send the claim for reprocessing?"

"No, you've already submitted an appeal, so there's nothing I can do."

"Okay, then we're going to keep billing the patient."

"If that's the case, I'm going to issue a letter to the provider, and contact Medicare."

"Okay," I said.

"So are you going to write off the balance?"

"No."

A week later, Aetna issued a payment for the claim. I realize that what I'm doing professionally is ethically prickly. That's why I'm working for the bigger site that pays over half-a-million dollars a year. Of course, my pay hasn't increased as a result.

Near the end of the day, I go to the bathroom and Wilson is looking closely at himself in the mirror as if worms are crawling through his beard. He sees me, whistles through his teeth, and waits for me to stand at the urinal before he leaves.

When I get home, my dad's car is parked in my spot. We haven't seen each other in a few weeks, but Lynn and I haven't felt like socializing. He's never come uninvited when I'm not around, though.

Before I get my key in the lock, Lynn opens the door and gives me a look. She probably had to let them in while she was wearing a robe, and spent the last ten minutes putting her hair up and changing clothes.

"I saw Dad's car," I say.

"They're both here," Lynn says.

Mom covers her mouth while Dad sucks air through his gritted teeth. I texted Mom that I had an MRI done and might need help with the bill if Cigna doesn't pay. I've had to ask her for money a few times since Lynn quit her job, so I'm always ready for Dad to try lecturing me or cutting me off. This might be it.

"Did Batman push you into a chemical vat?" Dad asks.

"I'd have a nicer place if I was the Joker," I say.

"What's happening?" Mom asks.

"Dr. Till doesn't know," I say. "They couldn't draw blood because the needles couldn't break my skin. That's why I had the MRI."

"And?" Mom asks.

"None of my organs are shutting down and I don't have cancer," I say.

"That don't explain your skin, son," Dad says.

"Could we all sit down?" I ask.

Lynn hides in the bedroom while my parents sit across from me on the couch. The dining room chair I'm sitting in wobbles like a see-saw. We bought our table and matching chairs from a couple in Rockmart for forty bucks.

"Has work said anything?" Mom asks.

"I still have my job," I say. "I don't know what else to do, guys."

"We'll see about getting you to a specialist or something in Atlanta," Dad says. "So, you might need to take some time off soon."

"You know, I don't think I want to do that."

"Don't you want to know what's happening to you?" Dad asks.

"I'm turning green," I say. "It might be temporary."

"What did Dr. Till say?" Mom asks.

"I already told you I'm not dying," I say.

"Why don't you go get your skin bleached like Michael Jackson?" Dad asks.

How do I politely tell my parents to leave me alone? I'm hungry and just got off work, so my brain feels like scrambled eggs. Dad might as well pick me up and shake me like a maraca.

"Do you want to get dinner?" Mom asks.

"You guys kind of blindsided Lynn," I say. "I don't think we can tonight."

"Is she going to get a job?" Dad asks. "What if you lose yours and can't work anymore because of this?"

"Me having a problem doesn't solve hers."

"Excuse me," Dad says. "How long has she been out of work? Six months? She needs to be a grown up and get a job for both your sakes."

"Alright," I stand up. "Nice visit. Good to see you. Bye."

"We're not going to just let you die with no support," Dad says.

"I'm not dying."

"Come on, Marion," Mom says.

Lynn comes out when they leave. She winces as if her stomach can't handle looking at me anymore. Usually she stares at the floor or over my shoulder to avoid eye contact with me now. If she ends up leaving me over this, I imagine even a lawyer with a soul won't see my condition as fair to her. She didn't marry a green man.

"I think he might be right, Wayne," Lynn says. "I'll apply to some jobs tonight after we eat."

"What will you do?" I ask.

"Not another call center," She says.

"I wouldn't let you do that again."

Chapter 3

We didn't meet at a party, because neither of us went to parties. Unlike my fantasies of bumping into my soulmate in the college library, Lynn preferred studying in her dorm, and she was a business major. A lot of people think business degrees are more worthwhile than an English one, but the truth is that most degrees are worthless unless they're in a specialized field. No, I met Lynn while waiting for chicken wings at Hairless Samson's Bar and Grill, which was open late for college students.

Despite the intriguing name, Samson's was a hole in the wall dive connected to a gas station. When the pumps shut down, locals would park under the awning. Instead of ambient lighting like a Jazz club or smoky bar, there were fluorescent lights and a narrow row of tables. I was sitting near the drink cooler when Lynn came in with her friend, Carol. I don't recall ever seeing Carol after that evening.

If we'd met in high school, and were the same age, it's unlikely Lynn and I would even acknowledge each other. She was a cheerleader and in the drama/chorus crowd. I wasn't involved in anything extracurricular, and certainly didn't think cheerleaders possessed any substance. Most high schoolers don't; including myself.

When Lynn first looked at me, I had the advantage of age and a decent two week beard. See, kids on TikTok and Reddit seem to think the dating world works against certain types or everyone within a certain bracket is trash. Redpillers and incels think women rule the world because the dating world is their buffet. However, they all conveniently ignore that we all like people who are older than us. If I was eighteen and a twenty-two year old woman looked me in the eye, I would've melted faster than burnt butter in a cast iron skillet.

So, when I smiled at Lynn, she smiled back. I waved with my two forefingers, and she waved back. I stood up to get my wings, introduced myself, and left two minutes later with her number.

Now, Lynn faces away from me in our bed and stares at her phone. Every time I go to pee or brush my teeth, my reflection spooks me as if an alien is hiding in the bathroom. Rather than showing signs of this condition going away, my skin grows darker. By next week, I expect to look like the Hulk if he ate a palate of laxatives.

"What are we going to do if this gets worse?" Lynn asks.

"You or me?" I ask.

"What?"

"Your depression or my transformation into an X-Men character?"

"Your skin thing."

"It is getting worse," I say. "I'm still the same person, though."

"What are we going to do, Wayne?"

"I don't have an answer to that question."

"Then go to a specialist like your dad suggested."

I haven't asked her how she feels about my change, and I initially wasn't concerned because I didn't think it affected her. A woman wouldn't leave her husband if he went bald, gained weight, or lost his arm in a zoo accident. I suppose those changes are expected of men as we're stressed and reckless about our appearance. Perhaps I should reach out to Lisa Marie for advice, but she was with Michael when he was white.

"If this is who I am from now on," I say, "Are you going to stay?"

"I don't know," Lynn says.

"You haven't been happy in a while," I say. "Seems like you need a change."

"I'm not unhappy with you," Lynn says. "I'm unhappy with everything."

Rather than dig deeper, I turn over and shut my eyes. I imagine Lynn feels what I've felt this year. I can't cure her depression, and she can't stall my change. Neither of us understands each other's afflictions. We can both tell one another, but that doesn't result in comprehension. Sometimes the more we speak, the more confused we become. What I know is that we're no longer secure in our marriage.

When we started dating, Lynn and I found out we were both only children to parents who never divorced. Such a concept is alien to half the population because their parents divorced when they were seven, and their daddy moved in with a woman eight years younger than mommy and stopped picking them up on weekends. Most marriages that last result in at least two offspring, so only children of married couples are rare. However, we both understood that such a relationship did not result in security.

Marion Pallidus studied theology at Emory and received his Master's degree in Divinity when I was three. Josie, my mother, still works as a regional salesman for Liver Industrial, a furniture company. She supported us while Dad finished his degree and received his ordination. Lynn's parents are atheists, so she didn't grow up with

God. This was the only major difference we spotted in our relationship in the courting phase.

Lynn was a rare specimen from my perspective because generational atheism isn't common in the South. Usually kids grow up like me and start thinking about their beliefs in their teens before rejecting what came before them. Lynn didn't even know I still believe in God until a few months ago when we were driving home from the local Mexican restaurant, the Lazy Donkey.

As I'm trying to fall asleep and these facts swarm my consciousness, I'm aware that they're meaningless right now. God isn't doing this to me no more than He is punishing Lynn for not believing in Him. I never bought that nonbelievers go to Hell. Dad has always quietly doubted Hell's existence. Why would God create a place to punish people when we're all so fucking stupid? That would mean billions of souls are suffering for eternity for ignorance while a handful of people get to dance in the clouds with golden harps. God doesn't need to punish us when our guilt and self-sabotage serve as punishment.

Lynn will eventually feel better. However, I don't know that I'll ever look the same. My face hasn't changed. My body remains in the same physical shape. But the first thing everyone notices about me is this green hue. They'll think I spilt dye all over myself or have some disease that they might catch.

When I walk into the office, people don't look up from the floor, and often hold their breath. This morning, I am looking forward to going through accounts and taking my mind off what's happening. That's my favorite part of this job. Tedious work is good for my mental health. Working claims isn't as tedious as wrapping silverware, washing dishes, or cleaning stock rooms, but that's the ethic I apply. One claim after the other without mentally pausing.

There's a box in my chair, and my photos of Lynn, the framed illustration of Darth Vader she bought me from Etsy, and Garfield Funko Pop are inside. My former cubicle looks like the other empty ones on each side. I sense that they're not moving me to another part of the building but rather out of the building altogether.

Miranda comes out of my manager's dark office and holds out her hand.

"May I have your badge, Wayne?"

She's wearing blue nitrile gloves and has a plastic bag.

"When did you make this decision?" I ask.

"It wasn't me," She says. "The home office in Atlanta called me this morning."

"So they know about this?" I gesture to my skin.

"I'm sorry, Wayne, but could you give me your badge and take your belongings?"

I drop the badge in the bag and turn to grab the box. If I knew Miranda wasn't going to escort me out, I'd be sure to stop by Kendra's desk for a final four-letter word. Now wouldn't be the best time to bring up my family's attorney and gloat about a wrongful termination lawsuit, which is going to happen, because I know corporate already weighed the cost of doing so before they called Miranda.

Once we're outside, Miranda looks around to see if anyone is around before straightening her posture and her forced smile dissipates.

"I am to offer you a severance package that will include the remainder of your due pay for 2019 along with insurance benefits, and I have to ask if you're willing to accept this before I send you the off-boarding documentation to your email."

"It's October," I say. "That's less than three months salary."

"If you don't accept, I have to inform corporate."

"And?"

"Come on, Wayne, you and I know they're screwing you. I still have to offer the severance. You'll still be paid for the remainder of the month even if you don't accept."

"Okay."

"So, off the record, I suppose I might be seeing you again pretty soon."

"I'm going home now, Miranda."

This office building was always a double edged sword of stress and a safe haven. Now I'm walking out of here for the last time, and I wasn't expecting to lose my job today. The severance that corporate offered me likely came with a contract that stated I couldn't file a lawsuit or work for a competing company within a certain time frame. They were essentially offering me less than six thousand dollars and the same shitty Cigna insurance coverage until 2020, and I might not be able to find a new job by then.

But Lynn and my parents wouldn't let me leave for something out of my control. Plus, I have enough knowledge of fraud within the company and providers offices that I could report them to CMS. I'd rather not be responsible for layoffs, though.

"Wayne?" Mom answers.

"Hey Mom," I say. "I'm in the parking lot at work. They just let me go."

"Are you serious?"

"See if you can get Florence Garner on the phone."

"Oh. Yeah, I'll call her right now. Is there anything I need to tell her?"

"I'm developing green skin, my PCP hasn't found anything life threating about it, and my company just fired me, so we need to file a wrongful termination suit."

"Do you think you can stop by Dr. Till's office for your records in case Flo needs them?"

"I'll head over there now," I say.

## Chapter 4

Judge Floyd's breathing fills the room as each attorney and myself sit silently. When he clears his throat, it shakes the table. Adjusting his glasses, he looks at my medical documentation and EHR Interactive's HR paperwork Miranda filed last week. Flo knows Floyd from UGA, apparently. Her father was a professor there, and Judge Floyd wouldn't be an attorney at all if not for him. Otherwise, the wheels would turn so slow it would be 2021 before I could get a hearing.

"This is going to be quick, y'all," Judge Floyd says. "I'm going to allow EHR Interactive's team to make their statement, we'll hear from Mr. Pallidus's representation, and we can do any rebuttals before a ruling. Keep it brief."

EHR Interactive's legal team are Jennifer Patterson and Melvin Lonnell, who would look like the number ten if they stood straight next to one another. I had email exchanges with Jennifer when there was concern over my former urological site not making their monthly payments for two months. She sounds more masculine than Melvin, who might pass for Oliver Hardy if you gave him a top hat.

"Our HR rep at the West Georgia branch contacted us regarding an employee with a potential health hazard," Jennifer says. "She reported that several employees were uncomfortable working in the same building as Mr. Pallidus, and it was his manager that stated she would no longer work for our company if he was kept onboard. We were unable to confirm the condition that Mr. Pallidus is suffering from and could not determine if it was contagious, but we decided it wasn't worth the hazard in office. We offered Mr. Pallidus a severance package that covered his pay for the remainder of 2019 including his health benefits, which he declined. Georgia is an At Will Employment state, and EHR Interactive was in the right to sever Mr. Pallidus's employment with the company."

"Did your HR representative speak to Mr. Pallidus's colleagues or manager regarding his condition?" Judge Floyd asks.

"She merely reported back to them what he told her that his condition was not terminal."

"So your HR representative told employees about his condition without his consent?"

"That was another judgement call on our part," Melvin says. "Mr. Pallidus's condition came on suddenly according to her report."

"I suppose I should point out the obvious," Judge Floyd says. "If Mr. Pallidus's illness was contagious, he may have caught it from your West Georgia campus. Have any other employees shown symptoms of this illness or been discharged as a result?"

"No," Jennifer says.

"Mrs. Garner."

Florence Garner married Jason Garner twenty years ago, and Dad officiated their wedding in our church. Jason is a deacon, and Florence sings in our choir, so any legal assistance the church receives is pro bono. Unfortunately, my case is not free.

"According to my client, Mr. Pallidus," Flo says, "He was a well-respected employee that worked for a multi-million dollar medical group in Virginia. Despite that he was able to handle a site he states made a lot of money for EHR Interactive, he received a one-dollar raised in late 2018 and has yet to receive any bonus or incentive for his services. Sounds like a very loyal employee to work to make so much money when he makes so little, no? He could've sought employment elsewhere with his qualifications, yet he remained with this company. I imagine with his sudden departure, this medical group is asking very serious questions regarding turnover and why EHR Interactive would let their best claims analyst go. This decision to release Mr. Pallidus could potentially cost them a lot more than the six-thousand or so dollars they would have to pay him in severance. Your honor, it appears this was a brash decision on their part and reactionary rather than precautionary. Mr. Pallidus was examined by a physician who determined he was healthy aside from his skin changing color. He even offered his medical records to their HR department for review, though they never formally accepted. Being let go from his position not only puts him at a disadvantage financially, but he also cannot find work elsewhere given his physical appearance and status as a terminated employee. His wife is currently unemployed, so he has to rely on borrowing money from his parents in the event he cannot find work in the coming weeks. EHR Interactive are punishing Mr. Pallidus for something out of his control, and he is suffering financially, physically, and mentally."

Judge Floyd looks at me with an expression of pity and disgust as if I'm a bleeding frog staining a creek bed. When he turns to Jennifer and Melvin, he pulls a peppermint from his coat pocket and pops the candy into his mouth. Melvin moves back in his seat.

"Do you have a rebuttal to this statement?" Judge Floyd asks.

"It was never our intention..." Melvin starts.

"That sounds like an apology," Judge Floyd spits. "I asked if you have a rebuttal."

"No," Jennifer says.

"Mrs. Garner, what damages do you seek?"

"Considering my client's inability to ever work again if his condition continues," Flo says, "Two million."

"That's sickening," Melvin says.

"You have the option to settle for an agreed upon amount," Judge Floyd says.

"We can offer fifteen thousand," Jennifer says. "That is roughly six months' pay."

"So Mr. Pallidus is supposed to continue living like an undervalued employee for half-a-year and end up on the street?" Flo asks.

"Mrs. Garner is right," Judge Floyd says. "Frankly, I think two million sounds too low."

"Five hundred thousand," Melvin slaps the table.

"This is not an auction house," Judge Floyd says. "Now, if you're unwilling to be realistic and waste more of my time, I'm going to cease these proceedings."

"We'd have to get corporate approval for more than what we originally offered," Jennifer says.

"Why is your corporate officer not here then?" Judge Floyd asks. "Alright, EHR Interactive has the opportunity to appeal this decision, but I'm ruling in favor of the plaintiff. I hereby order EHR Interactive to pay three-million-and-five-hundred-thousand in damages. This amount is taxable by the federal government and Mr. Pallidus's representation will likely be taking a cut in legal fees."

Judge Floyd signs a document, which he hands to the court reporter, who stands while he leaves to his office down the hall. Jennifer and Melvin don't make eye contact with us before exiting. Flo puts her hand on my shoulder and gives me a squeeze.

"Congratulations, Wayne," She says. "I have never seen someone become a millionaire so quickly before."

"Maybe it can fund the treatment for this," I hold up my green arm.

"Let me tell you," Flo says, "If God willed it, you better not try to reverse it. As long as you're healthy, I say buy you a house away from everyone and be whatever you wanna be."

The ride back home has me contemplating that I could die in a car wreck and never see a penny from EHR Interactive, and death would be preferable than going home looking the way I do. I could've won a hundred billion dollars, but I'm still an abomination. If the media takes interest in this case ruling, a lot more than a few people around town will hear about the green guy. I'm lucky my landlord hasn't found out yet.

Having that much money is dangerous for my marriage. Some people might think money solves a lot of problems, but Lynn might decide it's time to divorce me so she can take half of what I made and move to Oregon or someplace where someone else can make her happy. I might as well pack my things and move into my parents' basement today.

Lynn hasn't even woken up yet. I sit on her side of the bed and put my hand on her butt since she responds more positively to me gently waking instead of saying her name. Reaching for the lamp on the bedside table, she keeps her eyes closed and exhales as if she'd held her breath the whole time I was gone.

"Well?" She asks.

"The judge ruled in my favor," I say.

"That's good. How much are you gonna get?"

"We should probably talk about that when you're more alert."

Sitting up, Lynn brushes her hair back and presses against her temples. Those eyes resemble what a monster under the bed must look like to paranoid children.

"Do I need to keep looking for a job?" Lynn asks.

"Depends on whether or not you want to work," I say.

"You know the answer to that."

"Let's say it's enough money that we wouldn't have to work ever again," I say. "What are you going to do?"

"What do you mean?"

"Are you going to leave me?"

"Wayne."

"I know it's unfair of me to ask, but I want an answer."

"I think I need time to myself."

"Alright," I say.

"I think we got married really early, and I didn't really get to live life the way I was supposed to. I don't think I can do that if I go out in public with you."

"So, do you want a trial separation?" I ask.

"No. I should probably find my own place and see where I'm at."

"Well, it sounds like you need a job, then."

## Chapter 5

I wear a jacket, gloves, a Peanuts baseball hat, and sunglasses so nobody immediately freaks out when I step into the Douglas County Finance and Investment Center, which is next to the original courthouse downtown. With a name like this, I was expecting at least a two-story building. Instead, there's a receptionist desk and a single hallway that clearly leads to a break room with offices on each side.

Genevieve Arbor's office is the last door on the left, and she's currently eating gummy bears off a napkin while playing online chess on her phone. When I shut the door behind me, she looks up to see a man who bears a resemblance to the Unabomber and every police sketch ever before I take off my hat and glasses to reveal myself.

"Is your name Wayne?" She drops a bear on her desk.

"Yes, ma'am," I say. "I made my appointment under the name Edgar Poe, though."

"I've read more than one book in my life, sir," She says. "And I also read the news."

"Then you know I recently came into some money," I sit down.

Her hair reminds me of the way women used to wear blazers with big shoulder pads and knee length skirts in bank commercials. There was one with a cheesy "Sharing the Hometown Spirit" jingle, which I associate more with the early nineties than Nirvana. Genevieve is too young to remember such trivialities because she barely looks twenty.

"Do you mind if I ask your age?" I say.

"I'm twenty-three," She says. "Do I seem older or younger?"

"That's a trap. Would you believe me if I said I just turned twenty-eight?"

"When's your birthday?"

"November second."

"You look like you could be twenty-eight or forty-eight," She says.

"Wow, I didn't realize anyone could make me feel worse."

I wink to let her know I'm kidding, but Genevieve almost swallows her upper lip as she throws away the gummy bears and closes Microsoft Edge on her desktop.

"So, I'm here for two reasons," I say. "I need a house, and then we need to look at a safe investment for some of my money."

"Typically people go to a bank or realtor when they wanna buy a house."

"Most people aren't millionaires."

"Well, I do have access to Google and Trulia, I suppose."

"I can reimburse you for the extra effort," I say. "I need a mouthpiece for as many people as possible. You may not have noticed, but my skin makes me look like I'm cosplaying as the Jolly Green Giant."

"Okay, so what are you looking to spend?"

"The most important aspect is land. I don't want a farm, but I need enough coverage so that people can't see me if they drive by or look out their window. However, I also need a cable connection for internet, so it can't be in the boonies."

"That doesn't sound practical at all, Wayne."

She turns her screen to face me as she pulls up Google Maps and types in an address. It's a neighborhood I'm actually familiar with only five minutes from my apartment. Lynn and I would drive through there during Christmas to look at lights. There was one house that used to have a weird colored bulb in one room, and I assumed it was for either a goth kid or orgies. There're many empty plots, though it's hardly secluded. Anyone like me can drive around and gawk at the properties.

"I know this property because it's an investment safe haven," She says. "Every empty plot is owned by someone who has no intention of living there. It's not too costly, either. See this one corner over here? There's enough room to put a house here with a sturdy fence to keep anyone out, and..."

"I don't want to build," I say. "I don't have time. My wife and I are separating."

"Well, even buying can take time."

"I'm aware. I don't want to live over there anyway."

"Let's circle back on that," Genevieve says. "You wanted to talk investments."

"I'm aware that I have over two million dollars," I say, "But I need to make sure the money doesn't run out. This is supposed to last both my wife and I for our entire lives."

"You're married?"

"Separated," I say. "My wife is staying in our apartment until the lease is up in April 2020."

Genevieve scratches her chin while sizing up the information I just unloaded on her. I'm well aware my marriage is likely ending. The last real conversation I had with Lynn ended with her saying she didn't want to have sex with a man whose penis is green. We haven't spoken since. However, I believe that if we got married, I owe my wife something for her future.

"I recommend Fidelity," She says. "We can look at individual stocks, but Fidelity is going to be secure enough with a Roth IRA so you pay taxes up from and none of your accruals or withdrawals are subject to taxation."

"How much do you recommend?" I ask.

"I think it's smarter to keep your money fluid rather than in one place. Put some away in savings, a Roth, and a solid stock like Apple or Microsoft."

"If I give you a million dollars," I say, "Can you make that judgement for me?"

"You'll have to sign off on everything, and I think it's wise if I explain my decisions before I pull the trigger on anything."

"Fine," I say. "By the way, there's a place in Newnan I want you to look at for me. 1199 Bitterman Court."

I wanted to bounce ideas off her before giving her a definitive answer. There's a chance I won't get the property, of course. However, there's a small church in Newnan where my distant ancestors are buried, and I noticed the incomplete development nearby. A lot of times, a contractor or investor will try developing a subdivision and it fails before anything gets off the ground. The house popped up around the last time I drove by in 2019, and the remainder of the street is empty plots with scattered pine trees and For Sale signs.

"Oh, that's kinda secluded," Genevieve says. "Once all these lots are full, you're going to have a lot of neighbors."

"Try to get all the plots," I say. "It shouldn't cost more than five-hundred thousand."

"That's insane. I mean, I don't want to dissuade you from buying land, because land is always a smart investment, but this was zoned for a neighborhood. Five-hundred thousand is lowballing it."

"Offer them one-hundred for the house and the land, and another hundred for the remaining properties then. Let me know what the developer says. I imagine if they can't get anything sold or built by now, they're bleeding."

"I don't see it happening, Wayne."

"Humor me."

I walk to the courtyard in the back where city employees used to take smoke breaks. It's rare I get to sit in the sun anymore, and today its overcast. No one is around to gawk at me, though. Mom has to do my grocery shopping now that Lynn checked out of my life. Normally when people break up, they at least have hope that they'll either reconcile or find someone new. I can't imagine anyone wanting me now unless they have a weird fetish.

Genevieve pokes her head outside before joining me on the bench. I wonder if she has good or bad news.

"The developer filed for bankruptcy," She says. "Wells Fargo owns all that property now. Even the house."

"Were you able to talk to anyone about an offer?"

"I have to get in touch with the Newnan branch, but I looked at the public records for that property and you weren't lowballing at all."

"Sometimes I'm smart."

"Seems to me you're smart a lot of the time if you're not blowing all of your money on dumb things. It's wise to invest, Wayne."

## Chapter 6

Mom puts hooks on each of my ornaments as I put them on the tree. Dad has yet to stop roaming around the property surveying every inch. Before he even stepped foot on the property, he kept commenting about the cost of mowing all the grass. I bought a riding mower just for my lawn; the rest can grow as nature wills it.

Usually Lynn is doing Mom's job by giving me the multi-colored plastic orbs and telling me where there's a bare spot. I wasn't going to bother putting up a tree this year at all, but she insisted it would make me feel more at home. Thus far, I'm only missing my wife and replaying what she said about not wanting my green dick over and over. How are my parents not acting in total disgust for what I'm transforming into, yet my wife can't stand looking at me?

"You didn't buy a star for the top?" Mom asks.

"I did one year," I say. "It kept going lop sided like in *A Christmas Story*."

"Might as well buy you one of those leg lamps since you're living the bachelor life from now on."

"There're dolls for that now, Mom. For a couple of grand, I wouldn't have to sleep alone ever again."

"I reckon that'd be better than a mail order bride. I wonder if your father knows whether God thinks that's a sin or not?"

"The sex doll or the Russian bride?"

"Oh hell," She holds her hands up.

Dad finally lets himself inside and starts looking up at the high ceiling. Whoever designed this house was really trying to be unique, because it looks like a two story home on the outside, but most of the space is on the first floor. There's not a basement. Instead, the upstairs master bedroom has a door leading into an attic storage space. I'm sleeping on the ground floor in what is supposed to be a guest room. There's only a half-bath up there, and the nice tub is down here. I sort of imagined myself living in a cabin and splitting logs by myself, but I'm well aware of my limitations. Without internet and central heating and A/C, I'm basically Chris McCandless.

"Marion," Mom turns to Dad, "Are sex dolls a sin?"

"Is that like a voodoo doll?" Dad asks.

"Do you want the tour?" I ask.

"Oh, I saw the property," He says. "When are you going to get rid of that Escort?"

"Are we talking about the sex doll?" Mom asks.

"Get you one of them electric cars like an Edison."

"I think you mean a Tesla," I say. "And no. I'll probably buy a used Prius."

"We raised him wisely," Mom says.

She uses the word We quite liberally. Ministers, pastors, and preachers have two jobs. They're rarely just in the church business. When he wasn't behind the pulpit or in the office next door, Dad taught theology courses at the local college. Teaching is not merely showing up in the classroom, though. Grading papers and coming up with lesson plans also took up his time. Despite that Mom also worked, she didn't have to worry about her job once she left her office.

I mostly remember the dinners. Dad always dropped what he was doing to eat with us, and until I was about ten, he came to see me before I went to sleep. Between reciting Bible verses to chastise me if I verbally stepped out of line, Dad generally kept the conversation flowing with Mom.

When we went to the beach in Destin, my parents booked a room at the Holiday Inn for two nights, so we spent one day at the ocean, and generally ate Whataburger for each meal. But when we made the trek from the public parking lot, over the creaking wooden walkway, and to the sand, Dad stopped us before we took another step in the sand.

"Look at what God provided for us," Dad says. "He made us the beautiful ocean to gaze upon as a reward. It's a treasure, Wayne. When you work hard and save your money, you can take your wife and children here too."

I'm twenty-eight, likely to get a divorce, and haven't even had a pregnancy scare. Unlike my parents who maintained stable careers, provided a home for their son, and helped me well into adulthood, it took me changing into Swamp Thing and suing my former employer so I could buy a house. Someone lied to me along the way about how life was supposed to work, though. I worked hard, got a degree, married someone I love, and helped my wife when she needed me. For doing everything right, I know I must've done something wrong. Majoring in English or staying at a job that didn't value me. Not taking more risks.

Now, I spent a lot of money so no one will see me when I walk out into the front yard. However, I have a pantry now, so I don't need to worry about having too many cans of things I'll never eat. Mom brought me four cans of tuna because I've been stocking up for Lynn. I hate tuna.

Rather than standing outside with sweat glistening on my pine needle skin and an axe in my hand, I'm reading a Reddit thread while sitting on a rocking chair my parents gave me as a house warming gift. It's from Cracker Barrel. Lynn parks her Versa at the end of the driveway and waves with her index finger.

"Welcome home," I say.

"It's definitely a home," Lynn says. "Are you busy?"

"Just got off the phone with President Trump," I say. "He wanted me to be the MAGA mascot because someone told him about a man with American red skin. Sounds kind of racist when I say it out loud."

"Maybe you can marry a Fox News anchor. They're pretty hot."

Lynn sits on the white railing across from me and holds her hands under each arm as if she's cold, but it's seventy-five degrees today. Given her body language and lack of eye contact, I bet she's here to ask me to sign divorce papers.

"I put some money away," She says. "I figure if I'm going to ask you for a divorce, I should at least pay for our attorney."

"Wouldn't that be covered in a settlement or whatever?" I ask.

"I don't want anything from you, Wayne. Taking your money would make me forever indebted to you in some way.

"So, it's over," I say. "You don't want more time to think or consider that I am the same person you married?"

"Only with skin greener than the sod in Turner Field? There's nothing to consider. You can meet me at the courthouse in town tomorrow, and we don't ever have to see each other again."

"What the fuck, Lynn?" I ask. "If I'd contracted a gum disease and lost all of my teeth, would you divorce me then? If I was injured in a car wreck and unable to walk for the rest of my life, you'd leave? Those are rhetorical questions, by the way. I know you're not a mind reader, so I'd hate for you to think I expect an answer. You haven't considered what I'm dealing with given that every time I see my reflection, I make Steve Buscemi look like Brad Pitt. I've lost my job, I can't go to the grocery store, and my wife is rejecting me based on my appearance."

"Yeah, I know I suck," Lynn says. "Ten tomorrow, Wayne."

She's not fighting tears or walking away as if I said something hurtful. We might as well be strangers who accidently looked at each other at a red light.

"If my skin was white again, would you change your mind?" I ask. "Is this just the excuse you needed to leave?"

"I don't want to be married anymore," Lynn says. "There's too much I'm missing out on, and I'm not going to wait for you to change only to realize we weren't meant to be when I'm thirty-five."

With that, I realize I don't really know Lynn. She resents me for taking her college years when she should've been fucking up. Sleeping with more boys. Going to a few parties. We wanted to get married within a month of knowing each other. Such an attraction isn't rare at all. People want to tie down one another for the sake of procreation and fulfilling a societal role. Watching her drive away, I wonder when I'll wake up from this nightmare so I can have another chance. I'd like to know my wife a lot better. Maybe I could help her find the happiness she's missed this year.

If I don't go to the courthouse, what will she do? Maybe I should hire my own attorney. Such considerations are only selfish, passive-aggressive motives that result in more hurt feelings. Lynn said she didn't want to be married anymore, and she doesn't want to see me again. I suppose she was thinking about this before my skin changed.

## Chapter 7

"Are we still putting money away for Lynn now that she's out of the picture?" Genevieve asks.

There's a coffee stain on the white tile floor under Genevieve's desk, and I want to scrub it away, but I realize others likely tried and failed. Having left the courthouse this morning, I fixate on little things I normally wouldn't notice. There was a billboard with an attorney's face glowing under a guarantee you wouldn't have to pay anything until you won the case. A rip in the board right at the tip of his chin had me thinking he had a small beard. Seems like something Wilson would do.

"Yeah," I say. "Nothing big, though."

"We could talk about it later," She says.

"It's fine. What else have you got for me?"

"I have your Roth set up, and Fidelity submitted your taxable portion to the IRS. Apple was a little high this week, so I opted for Microsoft. I don't see them going out of business in the coming century."

"No Coca Cola?" I ask.

"We have some Diet Coke in the break room," She says.

"Stock," I say.

"Right now, it costs less than Microsoft, but it took a real dip in October. You want stability."

Yes, I do. Apparently, that means living alone and contemplating my failures as a husband until I break in some way. I might have to go to Dragon Con and pose as an alien. Maybe then I'll find my tribe.

"You need me to sign anything?" I ask.

"You did last week," Genevieve says. "That's why I asked about Lynn. That's the only thing I held off on."

"Cool. I would offer to buy us lunch since I haven't eaten today, but I don't think anyone will serve my kind."

"Are you a droid now?"

"I'm glad you caught the reference," I say. "I have a forty minute drive home."

"Why don't I grab us something and we can eat here? It's almost my lunch anyway."

I don't know of a more awkward option to eat than Chipotle when the only noise is the computer and florescent lighting. Every bite I take of my burrito makes me worry my chewing disgusts Genevieve. I loosen my muscles some when she takes a queso covered chip into her mouth and replaces all the other sounds in the room with her crunching.

"You from Douglasville?" I ask.

"My parents moved here from Smyrna when I was fourteen," She says. "Did you go to West Georgia too?"

"Yep," I say. "English major."

"I wanted to major in English, but my daddy said I oughta study something I could actually make money doing."

People are never shy about asking what English majors do with their degrees. The implication is that you can't do anything with a BA, and that implication is correct. We don't all end up working at Walmart, though.

"Are you gonna be alright, Wayne?" She asks.

"Each time I spoke to Lynn recently, she said something worse than the time before. It definitely gives me a lot to think about."

"What could you've really done to help?" Genevieve asks. "I doubt you asked God to make you look like Kermit."

"Miss Piggy never got mad at Kermit for who he was," I say. "I suppose this is the tradeoff. I get to live like a hermit with more money than I'll ever need, and everyone will leave me alone like I always thought I wanted."

"Oh, you shouldn't be sad. Lynn did you a favor. When someone leaves us, we should thank them for freeing us from a lie. My mama told me that everyone has problems, and you just have to find someone you like well enough to put up with them."

"So, you're saying I should start catfishing women," I say.

Genevieve has to hold her mouth shut while laughing so she doesn't spit Diet Coke on her desk. We have a professional relationship, but it's good to talk to someone. Maybe I should find a therapist.

"You can't live your life like Big Foot hiding from everyone or you'll become like that old witch in *Big Fish*. People will just make stories up about you until they'll be knocking on your door with torches and pitchforks."

"So I should carry on with my life as if I'm not a freak, huh?"

"Someone might think if you're a freak on the outside, you'll be a freak in the sheets."

"I don't like letting people down."

As I'm walking in the hall to leave, the receptionist comes out of the bathroom and looks directly at me. I smile and nod, and she waves, but backs away to her desk. As soon as I leave, she'll probably run to Genevieve's office.

I suppose I can test the waters by picking up some Coke Zero at Publix. There's a ten percent chance someone will shoot me, and even higher risk of someone trying to fight me. I'd like to see the statistics on an older lady screaming, though. The parking lot isn't too full, but there's always a steady stream of people coming and going.

Taking off my gloves and jacket, I roll up my sleeves and check myself in the rearview mirror. I'm still green. There's a baser part of me that is always surprised. Dr. Till never figured out why, and no one in recorded history has turned green and stayed that way. Then there was the whole thing with the needles not being able to penetrate me.

Last night, I cut up an apple I'd bought for Lynn. She never ate an apple whole. As if doing so made complete sense, I stepped to the sink to hold my forearm over the drain as I tried piercing myself. It felt like a cold edge slid on me like when I accidently walk too closely to a metal shopping cart. No blood. I tried stabbing my palm, and there was the same result.

I felt more sympathy for Lynn this morning when I signed the divorce paperwork. She wasn't there, of course. Her lawyer greeted me in the door, guided me to a desk with a notary, and explained to me there was nothing tricky about the deal. We were merely severing ties. Why would I fight the divorce when she didn't agree to marry someone who wasn't human anymore?

Even with the thought of people seeing me inside this store repulsing me, Lynn's memory dances around my head as if taunting me. I expect each shopper to stop to look at me as soon as I make my way through the sliding doors. Instead, they're all doing their thing. Each is a main character in their own story, and probably with someone analogous to Lynn who they loved but **couldn't keep.**

Sure, there's a man who does a double take with a polite smile that anyone might make if someone held rotten fish up to your mouth asking you to eat it. A little girl in a gray sweat suit walks next to her mother wearing matching clothes, and she pulls her child into the cart as if the floor is about to turn into lava.

When I reach down for a twenty-four pack of Coke Zero, a man with barely any hair and more wrinkles than a scrotum holds up his finger as much as his arthritis will allow to stop me.

"Is that makeup?" He asks.

"No, sir," I say.

"Oh," He says. "Did you notice that woman you just passed taking a picture of you with her phone?"

"You wanna help me hold her down to delete it?" I ask.

"I'm afraid you'll have to do most of the work. I'll stand guard while you do it, though."

He slaps me on the back and continues back down the other end of the aisle. I suppose the real test is waiting in line and letting a cashier ring me up. Publix still doesn't have self-checkout. I fucking hate this place. Everything is overpriced except their store brand, which everyone swears is quality stuff.

And they always have two or three registers open with at least one dumbass carrying a whole cart of groceries in the Ten Items or Less line. Unlike Walmart, Publix cashiers will usually tell customers to move to another check out. One advantage of looking like me is no one standing too close.

Yes, people give me a few glances, and there's always someone who doesn't have the social etiquette to not take a picture. Making a big deal out of someone taking your photo results in them taking a video. The reality we all inhabit is immune to rules we used to abide by.

"Oh," The cashier finally looks up to see who is next in line. "How are you today?"

"Freshly divorced," I say. "How are you?"

"Fine," She nods.

The bag boy's eyes might burn a hole in the counter top. He has a slight smirk as if he's going to start laughing if anyone speaks to him.

"How are you?" I say to him.

"Mmm hmm," He tucks in his lips.

"They call you Boomhauer around here?" I ask.

That's when he breaks, and the cashier's chin drops. I wink at the woman waiting in line behind me, who is equally confused as to how to react.

"Five ninety-eight," The cashier says.

"Think I could get some help carrying this to my car?" I ask.

"Uhh," She says.

"Yes, sir," The bag boy says.

This kid, who is probably seventeen and making nine bucks an hour, doesn't deserve a hassle for laughing at a stranger. I imagine he likes going outside, and he was the only one in the whole store who was honest about his feelings.

"What'd you first think when you saw me?" I ask. "You don't have to be coy."

"I had to look away and back again to make sure I was seeing right," He says.

"And?"

"I figured maybe you had paint on you."

"But then?"

"I never seen a green man before, so I kinda thought it was funny. You got a disease or something?"

"My doctor says I'm fine," I say. "I feel good physically."

"Your wife leave you over this?"

"Partly, yeah."

"Well, mister, I don't think that was very loving of her. Sorry about that. You have a good rest of your day now."

"You too."

## Chapter 8

One plus of having a large attic space is my tree can stay up here for a year and I'll forget about it until next Christmas. Mom and Dad gave me an Air Fryer, which gives me a reason to buy some frozen fries next time I go out. I gave Mom a Marc Jacobs purse and Dad a Marlin 1895, which I bought the same day I ordered mine. If I'm going to live next to nowhere, I need a gun, especially if I'm a walking target.

After they left, I took the tree down and laid on my couch a while without any noise from the TV or passing traffic. Silence is expensive. People deserve to experience Nothing after they lose everything. I know that I gained a lot. Mostly time alone. I would have that with or without the money.

I wouldn't say I'm depressed, and certainly not sad enough to stand between myself and fries. Dad's point about my car seems relevant considering Ford stopped making the Escort in 2003, and it's almost 2020. The funny thing about cars is that older and newer ones stick out. If you want to blend in, you need a car that's five to ten years old.

Admittedly, I hate car dealerships and salesmen. Another reason not to buy a new car. They're terrible investments too, because the fees added to the sales price with things like gap coverage, tailpipe lubrication, and hot oil injections, the value quickly drops compared to what you signed up to pay. Georgia also requires every driver to have insurance, which adds to the monthly bills. People are willing to pay for money pits, but not vote to use our tax money for things like public transportation or sidewalks that randomly end.

I'm also using more gas to get across town to avoid going to Publix again. Obviously, I'll avoid Walmart like any rational person, but there's a Crooks grocery store that seems like it wouldn't be super crowded near downtown.

A teenage boy with a pink Polo shirt stops in the parking lot and points at me.

"Hey, I've seen you," He says.

"And you see me now," I nod.

"No, I saw you on Instagram."

"I don't have an Instagram, so someone must've posted photos of me, huh?"

"Yeah, it was on Fuck Jerry's page."

"Is Fuck his first name?" I ask.

"Nah, it's a meme page. Hang on, let me see."

He scrolls on his phone until he arrives at a photo of me with white text that says: "When you got social anxiety but you gotta Dew the Dew." Someone even changed my Coke Zero into Mountain Dew, which is more insulting than the image. There are over sixty-thousand likes.

"You're famous man," He holds up his hand for me to slap.

"You want a selfie?" I ask.

"Oh fuck yes!"

If I normalize myself, even if people are laughing at me, maybe I'll decrease my chances of people assuming I'm the Creature from the Black Lagoon. He'll post this to his social media and hopefully his friends will think I'm a nice guy who doesn't eat children.

Crooks gives me former Piggly Wiggly vibes, though there's an old eighties song playing with the volume low enough to sound like its reverberating against the yellowing tile floor. Usually, the freezer aisle sticks out, but I have to go down a few rows to find the frosted glass doors.

They have Checkers fries, which sounds like a daring Air Fryer experiment. What am I going to have with these, though? If I get hamburger meat, I might as well get a basket to carry all this stuff in, or I could just make hamburger steaks, but I don't have any onions to sauté. As these meaningless considerations pass through my brain, which likely resembles a salad, a cart stops only an inch away from me.

"You need a cart, sir?"

She's bigger than the others who work here. I wouldn't call her fat so much as beckoning to the senses. Her hips definitely exceed the width of her elbows, though. With those blue eyes, no man would care if she was a string bean or Winnie the Pooh. That's why I'm immediately suspicious of her intentions. Someone is probably filming us, so I keep my eyes on her forehead.

"Thanks," I say. "You're a mind reader."

"Someone left it in the aisle over. You saved me the trouble of walking all the way back to the front of the store is all."

"Wayne," I offer.

"Somer," She says. "But it's not spelled like the season."

I turn around to see if anyone's behind me in the aisle. She looks so young she probably doesn't know about *Punk'd*, but douchebag kids love to prank people in public for internet clout. My paranoia is justified considering I just saw a meme of me buying soda only a moment ago.

"My name is spelled like the season," I say.

"Which season is that?" She asks.

"Spring because of all the Wayne. You know, April showers bring May Flowers."

She squeezes her nostrils and leans on the cart for a moment while a snort pushes through her laughter. The bad jokes always get the best responses, even if they're negative.

"How else would I get so green?" I say.

"Wow, I wouldn't have gone that far."

"Thanks again for the cart, Somer."

As I'm wheeling away from her, a song that sounds like the guy from the *Tarzan* movie starts playing, and my thumb taps along to the bassline on the shopping cart before I realize Somer is walking a little behind me to my right. She might just be headed in the same direction as me, though.

"You like this song?" She asks.

"Am I on camera?" I ask.

"There's a security camera on every aisle," She says.

"No, is someone filming us?"

"Did you see someone..."

I stop the buggy at the meat counter and look at this girl who is likely all of twenty years old, which means I was eight years old and could've held her in the hospital after she was born. I use that logic to justify why I would never date someone born after 1998 if I was single. And now I remember that I'm recently divorced.

"Do you have Instagram?" I ask.

"I could just give you my number," She says.

"No, I mean did you see the memes of me on Instagram or something?"

"Even if I haven't, how often does a green man walk past me in the store without looking back at me?"

"I imagine a lot of normal men look at you enough."

"Exactly."

There's a pause where she steps closer and looks around to see if anyone is watching.

"So, Wayne, do you want my number?"

"Wasn't I supposed to ask for that?"

"I have to go back to my register in thirty seconds, dude."

I hand her my phone and she inputs her contact information before calling herself so that now she also has my number, which will likely result in me getting prank and threatening calls all evening.

"You can text me to make up for not asking first," She says. "I get off at ten tonight."

Now I'm concerned about which line to go through when I need to check out. It'll be weird to let her check me out, but it'll be awkward if I avoid her. I also have to consider that texting someone her age has other implications. I'm uncertain of them, though.

My full freezer tells me I went overboard with all my ideas for what to put in my Air Fryer. Somer giving me the cart was a gateway to my inevitable weight gain. I suppose the chicken wings, tenders, and onion rings aren't so bad, but I got every variety of fry except sweet potato. Those taste what I imagine every old lady's vagina smells like.

It's probably best I don't contact Somer, especially because I can't trust every stranger's intentions. One day I'll be raking my leaves and someone in a black top hat will kidnap me and force me into their traveling circus. At least if I have a carny girlfriend, she won't have ulterior motives, especially if she has a beard.

My life is obviously full of excitement when the highlight of my year is eating fries while rewatching *Breaking Bad*. I usually binge the series once a year, and Lynn hid in our bedroom doing her own thing. She watched alongside me when we first moved in together, though. Back then, she didn't need her space as much.

At 9:58, my phone vibrates, and it's Somer saying "Hey." Through reflex, I text her back, "Hey!" The exclamation point probably scares her more than my appearance. She's possibly part of the circus master's plot to kidnap me and force me to fuck the five-hundred-pound lady. I'm not opposed to the sex so much as removing me from my air conditioning and privacy.

Rather than sending me a follow up text, Somer calls me, which is another red flag that I'm dealing with a calculating psychopath who will probably frame my skin like a tattooed Yakuza.

"I just got off," She says.

If it were Lynn saying that, I'd tell her I haven't gotten off since Tuesday. Such jokes might give her the wrong impression, though.

"You'll think I'm crazy for saying so, but I miss leaving work," I say.

"You don't have a job anymore?" She asks.

"Afraid not," I say. "I'll probably be a bum for the rest of my life."

"That's okay. You're braver than the rest of us. I always thought I'd be a famous singer and be on a tour bus sleeping all day."

"There are worse things to lie to yourself about."

"My daddy told me he's heard slaughtered pigs that sing better than me."

"Why did your Dad spy on you and your boyfriend like that?"

That's a joke that will probably make her hang up and tell everyone she knows about. It'll be in her Instagram Stories or a Reddit thread.

"Nah, I never brought a boy to my house," She says. "I got more sense than that, don't you know, Wayne?"

"My first girlfriend used to turn up the stereo in her room," I say.

"Was that back in the 1970's when everyone had an eight-track?"

"My parents were teenagers in the eighties, so no."

"You don't look much older than me, but that might be the green washing out your wrinkles."

"I'm sixty-seven, so you might be right."

"Oh, Daddy," Somer says. "Don't tease me like that."

"Everything I bought at your store today is about to come back up."

"Good, you can come eat with me. I'm fucking starving."

If I leave my house to meet a girl this late, I'm going to resemble a deer carcass ready to be butchered. Then again, I don't have much to live for, and my death might be a martyrdom people talk about for a few days.

"Do you cook?" She asks.

"You saw me buy a bunch of food," I say. "I don't have a chef, though now that I say it out loud…"

"That's what you get a wife for, Wayne."

"I had a wife, remember? Wait, did I say that to you or the other hot girl at the store?"

"You must've talked to a hot boy, because I'm the only girl there. Are you going to take my hint or do I have to invite you to my apartment where I have two roommates and sleep on a futon?"

"I live kinda far out," I say. "If I was secretly a serial killer, you couldn't get away and no one would hear you scream. A pretty girl like you needs to make more rational decisions concerning strange men."

"So you don't want to see me?"

Yes, I would like to glue your pubic hair to my nose and live between your thighs, but you're a bit young, and I'm green. As if society wouldn't frown upon our relationship enough. See, I always consider the endgame with women. Blame that on Dad. I had a one night stand with a girl from my film course in 2012, and that made the rest of the class tense since I had to avoid looking in her direction as she sat next to me for the entire semester.

"Come on," I say. "Yeah. You have to understand I recently moved here for the sake of privacy."

"Have your attorney draw up a waiver before I get there then."

"You know, you're pretty quick witted," I say. "I'll text you my address, but you'll have to call me when you get here so I can let you in the gate."

"My grandparents have a big fence, so I'm used to getting out to open a gate."

"No, this isn't that kind of gate. It only opens from inside the house or with my remote."

"So you're a rich bum."

I have all this money but don't own a jump rope. With this much anxiety about a woman coming over so soon after my marriage collapsing, I feel like I'm cheating. I run up and down the stairs a couple times, which only reminds me how out of shape I am from working an office job and suddenly being jobless.

If Somer was going to ambush me somehow, she'd have a van or Chevy Silverado following behind her. Maybe I should've told her about the rifle? The camera at the gate can only see so far. She could always text someone to come and let them in too. Loneliness is a dangerous emotion.

What if she's a Trump supporter and has a Confederate flag tattoo? I'd rather the van full of boys show up to prank me. Feeling all of this makes me want to call Lynn and cry. Losing my wife also ended my closest friendship. No one wants to grow up to have their parents be their own confidants. None of my colleagues wanted to keep in touch after I started changing. Deleting my social media has only further isolated me. It felt disingenuous to have my old photo on Facebook, and asking for trouble if I had a current one up.

Somer drives a Volkswagen Jetta, so a cashier has a nicer car than me. When Lynn came here, I might as well have bought a dirt pile to live in. Somer must've won the lottery before she came here.

"Your house is so cute," She announces before slamming her door.

"That was my top criteria for buying it," I say. "I would never live in a practical home, obviously."

"You got a house and a lot of land," She expands her arms. "Might as well be president."

"Speaking of presidents," I say, "Would you say ours is doing a good, fair, or terrible job?"

"You saying if I voted for Trump, you won't fuck me?"

"See, I wasn't sure if this was headed in the intercourse direction, but I will admit that I'd feel more comfortable in bed with a Bernie Sanders supporter than, you know, a person who thinks the Confederate flag is about heritage."

"You voted for Bernic?"

"I'd rather die."

"Well, I didn't vote in 2016 because I was seventeen. My birthday is November twelfth."

"Oh, I'm a November baby too."

Somer stands on my porch with her hands in each jean pocket while dramatically shivering as if the snowstorm of '92 made a comeback.

"Come in," I say. "We might as well see if one of us is crazy already."

Instead of allowing me to cook, Somer opens my freezer and puts one of my Salisbury steak dinners in the microwave. That's a smart move if she doesn't want me drugging her food. Coming here alone wasn't bright, though she probably told her roommates she was meeting the green guy from the internet. Law enforcement wouldn't need to look far.

"Those frozen dinners give me gas," I say.

"Me too, so get your clothes pin ready," Somer says.

"There's Smart Water and Coke Zeros in the fridge."

"I thought you were from the South?" She asks. "You don't got any tea?"

"Not unless you want Earl Grey or Sleepy Time."

I suppose now that we're not at her job, I can secretly gawk at her without being a creep. There was a woman I worked with at EHR Interactive that filled out jeans like that. It wasn't that I looked at her ass so much as her ass being unavoidable within a certain distance. I wondered if she could crush my pelvis, which would be the best injury ever. Somer isn't her size, so I won't find out tonight.

"Here," Somer puts her phone in front of me. "You can put this up if you want to."

"Why would I want your phone?"

"You asked if you were being filmed at the store. I kinda get that you're worried about that since you're all over the internet."

"All over?" I ask.

"I saw a video about you on TikTok this morning."

"Is that why you're here?"

"No, I'm here because I'm hungry and really like Salisbury steak."

"Keep your phone," I say. "For your own security if for nothing else."

"Please, Wayne, you're not going to hurt me. Although I've always fantasized about being on Dateline."

The kids are talking about me. Someone made a video about me. I know if I ask Somer to show me, I'll ruin the evening by obsessing over something out of my control. When I went to Publix, I knew the risks involved outcomes worse than going viral online. The concept didn't cross my mind, though. Despite that I am different than everyone, I feel wholly human. No different than when I was working in a cubicle and going home to a despondent partner.

While I hope one day my forgetfulness about my condition may lead others to ignore my differences, adversity binds people together. Groups form based on hatred of others. A common enemy makes for closer friendships.

If Somer actually wants to have sex with me, there's a possibility she'll be forever marked as the woman who fucked Gumby. That's part of the issue with our age difference. Though I'm not an old pervert, I'm mature enough to realize when I'm about to make a mistake. She's not an eighteen year old girl fresh out of high school, but adulthood isn't a certificate we receive when we turn a certain age. Wisdom often comes through trial and error, and I wouldn't want to serve as a lesson she learns.

I'm not all logic and analytics, though. I wanted her before I even saw her face. Beyond her body, the kind gesture and conversation made me feel good. She wasn't treating me like a novelty. The other people in my life who haven't rejected me have their reasons, but none of them are pure. I think my parents believe I'll get better one day.

What I realize is that if I am well on the inside, my skin doesn't represent an illness. I merely changed.

"Do you have work tomorrow?" I ask.

"My shift starts at three tomorrow," Somer says. "You'll be tired of me long before then."

"Self-deprecation is my personality," I say. "Get your own. I ask because I'd like to talk more. It's late and I don't want to keep you too long."

"I'd be lying if I said I didn't have a few questions."

"Sure," I say.

We move to the living room where a paused Bryan Cranston is in mid monologue. I turn off the TV having realized he was behind me the entire time Somer was eating.

"You didn't mention your wife when we met, by the way," Somer says. "But you did speak of her in the past tense, so I assume she's no longer your wife."

"I guess the divorce counts as my Christmas gift to her," I say.

"Christmas was yesterday," She says. "The ink hasn't even dried on your divorce papers and you're out hoeing around already?"

"I don't drink, so I have to find another way to forget her."

"Considering you're the color of a Heineken bottle now, I assume you cheated and beat her all the time right?"

"Did my teardrop tattoo give me away?" I ask.

"I'm sorry you're going through all that, Wayne. Would it make you feel better if I told you I don't find you repulsive?"

"Marginally."

"Having sweet tea would've helped you some, though."

"That's a lot of sugar," I say. "A lot of carbs."

"Use the fake stuff that gives you cancer then. By the way, am I going to get throat cancer in fifteen years if I suck your dick?"

"Not from one time," I say. "It's like cigarettes. You have to do it for three decades and endure multiple recessions before cancer sets in."

"You probably think I have some weird kink," Somer says. "I have a lot of weird kinks."

"Are you into feet or something?" I ask.

"I'm all talk, baby. I really haven't taken my VW around the block too many times."

The way she looks off makes me picture a cigarette in her right hand as she exhales a cloud of vulnerability. Somer is a twenty-one year old woman living in Newnan, GA. She probably has conservative Christian parents and still goes to church to see her friends. Maybe all of her talk was a shield she holds up for boys. The truth is that men are intimidated by lustful women who know what they want, because they have expectations. Men who pretend to chew nails for breakfast don't want to disappoint an experienced woman. That gives *them* the power. The boys driving around in their Silverados are on the prowl for the naive breed that won't question them. Sensible people don't give a shit about disappointing each other after fucking.

"I won't be insulted if you need to go," I say. "But you're welcome to stay."

Somer moves closer and touches my face with her short fingers and manicured nails. Her kiss reminds me of my early experiences kissing girls when we were afraid to break one another. There's a tenderness there as if I'm peaking at a gift I'm not supposed to open. It might be for someone else.

"The people laughing at you can't feel what I'm feeling now," Somer says. "I haven't seen you as being different than me since you talked to me today. You're just a man."

This is not what I need to hear after my wife left me, though I want to hear more. Somer seems like a sweet person and makes me want to abandon all apprehension. Another issue with her age is what haunted me throughout my marriage. Settling down or being attached to someone takes time away you can't get back. I wouldn't want her resenting me for what she perceived as a waste.

She sits up and uses her nails to run through hair which may or may not actually be hers.

"Can I see you again?" She asks.

"Hm," I say. "I'd like that."

"We can wait until the new year," She says. "Next Thursday?"

"Sure. What do you want to do?"

"I bet if we eat out, someone will take our picture and it'll be everywhere before we come home."

"I could actually cook for you this time," I say. "You can ask me more prying questions."

"I'll text you then."

Chapter 9

Amazon delivers my Kindle in the mailbox, which I am oddly enthusiastic about checking. Am I sixty-four now? When the fencing company put the gate up, I requested a metal door that would lock and unlock based on the internal clock. If I receive a package or junk mail, the deliveryman slides the door up and it locks sixty seconds after it drops back down. There's another door on my side of the gate, but it's on a hinge, so I don't have to worry about keeping it open as I gather my mail.

However, I wear a ski mask and gloves while walking up the driveway so no one sees my skin. Traffic is rare on this road, but someone noticing where I live won't end well. If I piss off Somer, she could post my address online. I might have to move to another state all because I was lonely and horny the day after Christmas.

Now that I have nothing but free time, now I can catch up on reading everything I wanted while using work and sitting on the couch doing nothing as excuses. I know I'll probably default to playing Pokemon on my Switch or Grand Theft Auto on the PC I splurged on, but I was an English major. Paperbacks tend to gather dust in a pile or on a shelf, and bookmarks are a blemish on the experience. There was a period when I dog eared pages. Hearing Sean Connery scold Rob Brown in *Finding Forrester* ended that habit.

Really, I'm killing time until I see Somer again, and I almost assume she's going to change her mind. Not having sex with her gave me both a sense of relief and disappointment. I can still back out of this without irrevocably hurting anyone's feelings.

Since I moved to Newnan, I'm closer to Dungeon Comics, which is the only other bookstore aside from Barnes and Noble. I bought some trades there last year before they moved further away from Big Lots, so I haven't seen the new store. Surely a bunch of Magic the Gathering nerds will act less repulsed by me?

Maybe I'll convince Somer to pick me up some Sprayberry's Barbeque soon, because I definitely can't go back there. There're two other BBQ places near downtown that never scratch the same itch as that vinegar based sauce and the thick Brunswick stew.

The parking lot is a little too big for a comic shop, though I know the place fills up during card tournaments. Looking at any comic and card store's social media is a traumatizing experience with photos of neckbeards and children sitting at long tables filled ass to ass. I had Pokemon cards as a kid that I traded with friends, and I eventually found a Charizard and lost interest because we were all building up to that one. I can't imagine a kid caring that a card was worth fifty-bucks now, but that seemed like gold to us in 2000.

An older guy with thick glasses and an awkward haircut sits behind the counter watching *Golden Girls* on his laptop. He glances at me before turning his entire upper torso around to make direct eye contact.

"Hi," I hold up my hand.

He curls his lips as if he wants to speak, but his vocal cords seize. I move on to the shelves where trade paperbacks sit in alphabetical order based on the publication. Batman is my first stop.

"How you doing?"

Another man approaches me, and I think he sold me the comics I bought at their former location.

"Curt," He offers his hand.

"Wayne," I say.

"You looking for anything special?" He asks. "We just got in some new merch on the other side of the store if you're into Funko Pops or collectables like that."

"I'm just looking at Batman," I point.

He tilts his head as he looks at me closer.

"You know, I wasn't sure if you were the guy I saw on Facebook or you're cosplaying as Martian Manhunter."

"No, this is my real skin," I say.

"Cool. If you end up deciding on anything, I'll give you a discount at the register. Let's say twenty percent. We're pretty dead after Christmas."

"Thanks."

Having found nothing interesting for Batman or Wolverine, I take a look at the other side Curt mentioned, and there's a shelf with rows of action figures. There's a large McFarlane Bane with the old *Knightfall* mask next to Tim Sale's Batman from *Long Halloween*. Even though I have money to burn, I still have the mindset of when I was making fourteen an hour. They're not cheap, but they would look cool in my house. Should I get one and wait for the other? It's not like I'm saving money from a newspaper route. If I buy one, I might as well get both.

I settle on a metal suit Batman Funko Pop and head to the register. The *Golden Girls* guy is watching me.

"Don't mind Barry," Curt says. "You ever read *Dark Knight Returns*?"

"Yeah, that's where that suit is from," I say.

"I don't think its good business to quiz customers, but I'm always curious."

"I mean, I'm not super into comics. Like, I couldn't tell you anything about the Fantastic Four or Green Lantern."

"There's a reason Batman is more popular."

Barry turns to look out the front window after someone arrives. Curt exchanges some kind of telepathic message with him before handing me my bag. After that, Curt and Barry are done with me, so I go outside to see a man a little too handsome for the Dungeon Comics crowd.

In undergrad, I had an African American literature professor who offered one extra credit assignment, and I was the only student who took the bait. Robert Bly, who is very much white, wrote *Iron John*, which I periodically remember because Bly not only defines archetypes and tropes of masculinity, but also the ridiculous parameters many men can't live up to. One of those is hair serving as a measure of a man. Mythologically, that makes sense thanks to tales from religious texts. Samson and Delilah come to mind.

I'm confident this man is ten years older than me, but he has thicker hair than me when I was in high school. Meeting him in an open space like this reminds me of Hans Landa pulling out his ridiculous pipe while sitting at the farmer's table in *Inglourious Basterds*. There's a Big Dick Energy contest without even speaking to one another. Those teeth with absolutely no space and a slight overbite tell me he's not here for comics.

"Hi," He says. "Steve Sebastian. It's Wayne, right?"

"Wayne," I nod.

"I'm a journalist of sorts. Actually, I come to Newnan whenever there's a movie or TV series filming here, so this is a little unique for me. I assume you've seen how popular you are on social media."

"Are you wanting to interview me?" I ask. "I have time if you want to sit down with me for a minute."

"Oh yes. Certainly."

I crank the Escort so the heat comes on, and Steve has an iPad in his lap with the Voice Memo app on. Curt and Barry are watching from inside the comic shop, so I assume one of them called him. I bet they met at the Circle Jerk Convention in Atlanta.

"Anything I ask you can refuse to answer," Steve says. "I'm not going to upload the audio of this recording to any online format, and I do not use iCloud. I work for the Associated Press, so don't worry; I'm not a MAGA nut job."

"Mmm hmm," I say.

"Do you mind if I print your first and last name?"

"Wayne Pallidus," I say.

"Oh, I know that. I read up on your lawsuit against EHR Interactive. It's the only case in history that involved someone with green skin."

"What do you want to know, Steve?"

"First, a little on your background. I assume your parents aren't green too."

"Yes, I am very unique in my transformation."

Right now, I want to drive away and have Steve fall through my car like a ghost. His demeanor tells me that he's going to ask me questions that make me out to be a freak. I can't deny that I'm different than everyone else on the outside, though.

"My father is a minister," I say, "And my mother is a saleslady. I went to University of West Georgia for a Bachelors in English, which is a very middle class thing to do."

"Why English?" Steve asks.

"I like reading. I always made A's on my essays in high school. I never really figured out what I wanted to be when I grew up, so I guess God decided for me."

"Are you a practicing Christian? Do you hold this condition against God?"

"No to both questions," I say. "I believe in God. I'm not convinced Jesus ever existed, but I accept the symbolism of the death and resurrection. Otherwise, I sleep in on Sundays."

"From what you've told me, it seems like you're kind of directionless. I don't mean that in a bad way. Most people don't ever figure out what they want out of life."

Rather than respond, I open the tin of Altoids in my cup holder and pop a couple of mints in my mouth. I know from podcasts that when the interviewer stops asking questions, they're trying to pull their subject into the false sensibility that they're relating or friendly. One should never answer a question if there's nothing being asked of them.

"Uhh," Steve says. "What I'm getting at is: Do you think this was triggered by stress?"

"I certainly had my share of stress when this started," I say. "My wife and I recently divorced, but the truth is that our problems started before I changed. My skin was a catalyst for her to ask me to sign the dotted line."

"Do you feel abandoned by everyone in your life?"

"My parents are still friendly with me. No one else from my past reached out."

"So when you see yourself turned into an internet meme with people laughing at your expense, obviously that adds to your alienation."

Again, I clear my throat and pretend that I'm ignorant enough to not know what to say unless he asks me something.

"If someone were to make a documentary film about your life right now, do you think it would be a harrowing story or kinda boring?"

"Very boring," I say. "Interesting question. Social media is acting like a documentation of all our lives, even if we had to delete all of our accounts due to a health crisis in our life."

"Do you resent all of this?"

"No," I say. "Everyone should go through something like this so they know who really has their back. Like the resurrection, everyone deserves a second chance no matter their sins."

"Is this retribution for something?" Steve asks.

"I must've really pissed God off if it is."

"Nice," Steve nods. "Can I get a picture of you for my story?"

As Steve gets his camera from the Audi rental he drove here, I take off my shirt and shoes before climbing on top of the roof, which deforms slightly under my weight. Rather than questioning me, Steve backs away to get Dungeon Comics in the shot. My hands grasp my hips with my elbows bent in such a way that I look like I belong on a comic cover.

"Think I could get one with you flexing?" Steve asks.

There's not much to flex, but I hold up my right bicep with my fist pressed against my forehead.

"Maybe one up close," He says. "You can keep your shirt off."

## Chapter 10

December 29th: The last Sunday service of 2019. I haven't been to church since I started college in 2010. No doubt that Dad mentioned his lost son on several occasions. However, today is the first time he invited me rather than prompting me to attend church, and the more people I normalize myself around, the less will think of me as a Spiderman villain.

It took me thirty minutes to get dressed. I'm fortunate to own more than one suit, though I do stick out a little since it's a tan beige blazer with khaki slacks rather than black, grey, or navy. Odd that I'd think my clothes make my appearance more apparent. No one is reacting to my suit.

Grabbing a hymnal from behind the front pew, I sit down near the Gibsons, who were in their seventies when I last saw them. Even with their glasses on, they probably don't recognize me as Pastor Marion's son.

The organ commences services at eleven, and the choir master leads the singers in "Because He Lives." Dad approaches the pulpit in his Goodwill suit with the same brown leather Bible he slammed on our kitchen table during lectures about my behavior. He's already opening his mouth to preach when the last note plays.

"We're surrounded by family and friends today we haven't seen in some time," Dad says. "Seems like every year during the holidays, people start feeling guilty and want to come home. This building is just that. Not a home. The people, the congregation make it a home."

Per usual, there's someone saying Amen in response to Dad's opening declaration. How long until he starts dissecting an entire book in the Bible? I must give him credit for not cherry picking verses like some ministers. He's very much like an English professor reading and interpreting rather than making his sermon all about our flaws or how we should live.

"However, y'all know me. You know my wife. You also know my son. Now, Jesus spoke the word to show us the path to perfection. Lives free from sin. When I stand before you each Sunday, I'm not up here to tell you I'm perfect or that no one is perfect. I atone for my misdeeds like anyone else, but you must ruminate on them. Stop sinning. You don't have to lie, covet your neighbors, cheat on your spouse, or hurt others. Nobody forces you to do those things. I didn't come up here to say my son is a sinner. He is a good man, but he is his own man. Some of you likely looked at him this morning but didn't recognize him. He's been gone almost a decade from our congregation, and I invited him back for everyone's benefit as well as his own."

I knew he'd call attention to me, and likely embarrass me. At no point in my adult life has his demeanor toward me changed. He's still a distant person who I don't know well. What I know of him is through God, I suppose.

"Wayne," He looks at me. "Will you stand in front of the stage over here?"

This is why I came, yet I feel like running out the side door. Such a move would likely get my ear chewed off over the phone later. Unlike my interview with Steve Sebastian, I keep my clothes on and stand before the congregation. Dad is smart to keep me on the floor with everyone to maintain the mentality that we're all equal.

Most of them look at me as if Dad dropped a cow carcass from the ceiling and splattered blood on their faces. His breathing fills the silence as they fear their gasps or mumbling may anger him.

"This is the same Wayne you knew before," Dad says. "Yes, this is my son. The same one many of you held when he was barely able to open his eyes. Y'all watched him grow into a man and leave the church. Now that he's back, I expect you all to look at him with an open heart. I'm not asking. He is still a child of God. We must not look at what he experiences as a tragedy but the same test we all endure from Him. He is not special, folks. Any one of you could wake up and lose something you had only eight hours before. Men, you've all looked in the mirror a little longer than usual and noticed the gray at your temples or thinning near your forehead. Are you less of a man just because you're bald one day? This person standing in front of me is a man no matter what he looks like. Do not think of him as suffering an illness as he is not contagious or a carrier. Wayne is our brother. Everyone, please rise."

As the congregation obeys Dad, he walks around the pulpit, puts his hand on my shoulder, and kisses my forehead.

"Gather around him. Touch your brother and know that he is human like you."

The Gibsons arrive first with a stream following behind. They place their hands on my other shoulder. The Marshalls follow suit by taking my right hand. In only a moment, I am covered in people's grasps as they try accepting me as their peer. Though I do not feel God's presence, my eyes water as each person expresses a sincere intent.

"Wayne," Dad says, "We all love and accept you."

When the sermon ends and the choir starts singing again, I go to the hallway leading to the bathrooms and small stairwell. As I'm opening the door to exit, Mom sees me as she leaves the ladies room.

"He scare you off that quick?" She asks.

"No," I say. "I just want to get out of here before Sunday traffic starts."

"I guess it is a bit of a drive back to your place. You don't want to come by the house for lunch? I have a roast and potatoes."

"Next time," I say.

She comes over to hug me, and I realize I haven't touched Mom since she first saw my skin changing. While Dad didn't give me much affection, Mom certainly babied me most of my life. I need more of that affection in my life, and I'm just now realizing that it's a necessity rather than a desire.

"I love you, son," She says.

"Love you too," I say.

Getting attention, being around people, hearing an organ fill a room, and voices all around creates a sharp contrast to the hum of my Escort's vents. I'm the only one in this parking garage, and I'm eager to get out because I can't go running back to that church because I suddenly feel alone.

If Lynn called me now and asked me to reconcile our relationship, I'd likely drive to our apartment now. The woman I love is no longer the woman she is, so I can't go back to what we had when our home broke before she wanted me to leave. The divorce and changes in my life aren't the painful part. Knowing that I'll never experience waking up to her asking me to hold her, making her laugh, hearing her whine for a forehead kiss, and all the things that made us feel like a couple rather than two people sharing the same space. Lynn wants us to be strangers now, but we almost perfected that this year while still married.

And when I sit at the red light at the Newnan crossroads leading to either the turn I make to my home or Crooks, I look at Somer's contact in my phone wanting to text her. If I wanted her badly enough, I could ask her to quit her job and move in with me today. There's a chance she'd do it. That wouldn't be to her benefit but rather a Band-Aid on my true disease. Eventually, she'd realize I wasn't interested in her as much as I was in healing a wound too quickly.

Today, Dad preached about Job, which I not only had to listen to multiple times in our house, but also in my World Literature course in 2012. After reading *Epic of Gilgamesh*, my professor assigned us Genesis and Job.

I take issue with much of the Christian Old Testament interpretations that take no heed of Jewish tradition. A huge chunk of the Old Testament follows the Jews and their plight with Jerusalem, so automatically assuming the serpent in Genesis is Satan and threading that into the Satan that appears in Job creates unnecessary conflict.

Why would God listen to Satan and allow him to destroy Job's life to prove that this random man truly believed in Him? Christians can't seem to even agree on the nature of Satan. Some describe him as a fallen angel. A common Jewish take on *Book of Job* suggests Satan and God are two sides of the same coin. I believe Christians blame Satan for Evil in the world because without an entity that represents Hell, disease, murder, and deception, then humans have to take responsibility their own sins. Also, what kind of loving God would create a place to put fallible souls who make mistakes in their life without any chance for redemption? I never hear God tell anyone they deserve damnation. That comes from Christians who want to see themselves as superior to others because they're "saved," when judgement itself is a sin.

The other aspect of Job, or even Abraham and Isaac's story in Genesis, that I find problematic is that God would ruin someone's life to the point of killing the innocent. Not only does this place the blame for every bad thing that happens to us as a test from God, but also points toward God as directly responsible.

Clearly, there's a biological reason why my skin turned green. To suggest that God chose me to punish also implicates Him as culpable for children with cancer or old ladies ran over by busses. Bad shit just happens. They're not tests.

## Chapter 11

Thursday should feel like Christmas because Somer wants to see me again. Instead, this feels like an obligation that I put off until the last minute because I shouldn't pursue a relationship with her. I very much want to, but I'm partially aware that's because I'm starving and she looks like a ripe peach that will drip their juices all over my chin. Twenties are the new teens in some respects, so I'm eighteen and she's eleven in comparison. Maybe that should be my new analogy to explain age differences? When I was old enough to buy tobacco and porn, as well as vote for Gary Johnson in the 2012 election, Somer wasn't even a teenager yet. I would've been put in prison and on a list once I got out for child molestation. However, I can't look at her as a child now no more than a sixty year old could see a thirty year old as a baby.

Kissing her made me feel good yet guilty. Even if she was a year older than me, the innocence in her remains undamaged by any man. I don't buy that she hasn't had sex, but there's a difference in two inexperienced teenagers exploring each other and an older person actually making you orgasm. Not that I'm an Adonis or stallion, but I'm more experienced than the boys in her age group.

I lost my virginity at fifteen, which I consider too young. Cassie and I weren't even dating. She was the one girl at school who had a Pixies shirt, yet wasn't popular with most boys because she wasn't as developed as an upper classman on the cheerleading team. Let's face the truth: Nobody wants to date someone in their own grade. Senior boys preyed on the new freshmen girls, which I still find gross despite that their ages aren't drastically different. No, Cassie was a friend who offered to help me satisfy curiosity if I helped with hers.

Two weeks later, we stopped talking and admittedly I was the reason. She wanted a temporary experiment before we branched out with other people, and I wanted Cassie to be my girlfriend because I started thinking I loved her. I have always been quick to think I loved someone. Had Somer stayed a couple hours later, I might've said it to her.

But my first time was terrible. Sex education doesn't tell you about the actual act. For instance, a male needs an erection in order to put a condom on. He also needs to be hard in order to enter a vagina. It doesn't just slide in, either. Sex without proper foreplay is a chore, and it's nasty. The different liquids and smells that happen made me second guess doing it.

Eventually, a person learns how to stimulate their partner before actual coitus. I mean, we've all heard about Pound Town, but the detour into Flavor Town is necessary and makes things actually fun. I've even ventured to Chocolate Town, which coincidentally is one of my favorite Ween songs. There can be some overlap between Pound and Chocolate Town, but those experiments failed almost as soon as they began for me.

Point being that if an older woman had taken my virginity, and hopefully when I was eighteen for her sake, I would've came within thirty seconds and she wouldn't get anything out of it. Assuming Somer has driven her Jetta around the block a couple times, she hopefully won't starfish like a pillow princess if we do have sex, though I'm wondering if I'm going to break something in her psyche. Will I be a regret or someone putting her on the wrong path?

I text Somer to see if we're still on for today. She asks if there are any foods I don't like with two heart emojis. I say I'm not a picky eater, even though I definitely have preferences, though no food allergies. She texts back that she doesn't eat fish or very many vegetables, but she learned how to cook steak from her mom. So that confirms she has parents and wasn't hatched from an egg. If I pursue a relationship with Somer, her parents will eventually have to meet me.

It's at three in the afternoon that I realize I haven't cleaned my house since she was here last week. Granted, I'm a bachelor and don't make messes, and I have a hardwood floor. All I need to do is run my Swiffer around the place, wipe down the countertops, make sure my Calphalon pans are clean, and pour bleach down the toilet. I did all the cleaning when I was married to Lynn, but she wouldn't clean up after herself. She'd spill Coke on the rug and I was the one to drop a towel down to soak up the soda so it wouldn't stain.

My yard also needs cutting, and I've never used a riding mower before. I spent the extra money for a Ryobi so I wouldn't have to worry about gas or oil. However, my actual yard might take more than an hour to mow. Then I look out my window, see that the grass is brown, and realize I spent three thousand dollars on something that's going to sit in my garage for two more months.

I'm sure I'm neglecting something that will scare Somer away. Then again, if my skin doesn't frighten her, what's another minor external flaw going to do? Turn her on more?

She might find something about me she doesn't like, though. That might be her best out. People never show their true selves this early in a potential relationship.

Somer arrives with two grocery bags and *Pretty Woman* on Bluray, which is something I didn't think existed. Sure, you can find that movie on DVD for a dollar, but in high definition? Must be her favorite film of all time. Most people don't even buy movies anymore.

"Did you work today?" I ask.

"I asked for the day off," Somer says. "I spent all day getting ready, you know?"

Her outfit is a pair of black leggings, white crop top, and a thin zip up hoodie that likely doesn't keep her warm at all. However, her hair is perfectly straight and there's not a blemish on her face. Somer is like an Instagram model that decided to slum it in rural Georgia for the holidays and got stuck.

"I just got dressed half an hour ago," I say. "I have this natural green glow."

"And bitch you are slaying," Somer says.

She walks past me to go inside, and tosses the movie on the bar next to the island before holding up the pan I set out for her as if proud that I thought of her. Once she reveals the potatoes and steaks, I know this isn't going to be something she throws together.

"Should I peel and slice those potatoes?" I ask.

"Oh no, honey, you just sit there and look pretty. Tell me about your day."

"Well, I woke up, texted you, brushed my teeth, cleaned up around the house, paced in my living room for a while, and now you're here."

"What do you do for fun?" She asks.

"Get lost in existential thoughts and disassociate from reality until something happens, usually. Sometimes I watch TV to pass the time before I have to go to sleep."

"We need to find you a hobby."

"When I worked, I didn't have to worry about passing the time," I say. "I couldn't get a job now if I tried."

"Does all your money come out your ass since you're green?"

"All of my money came from a wrongful termination lawsuit," I say. "According to my financial advisor, I'm making money from Microsoft stock and losing it again the next day."

"You should start an Onlyfans," Somer says. "I would, but I don't want to make fifty-k and have to explain to my daddy why I don't have to work at the supermarket no more."

"What's Onlyfans?" I ask.

"It's a site for lonely men to pay for women's nudes and talk to them. A few women are cleaning up on there."

"The internet is full of free porn. Not that I'd know."

"It's the experience they're paying for. To feel like they know you. They can request specific stuff, and if they're willing to pay enough, the girls do it."

"Like you, I don't want to explain to my dad, who is a minister, why I'm bringing in thousands of dollars from green dick pics."

"So it is green," Her voice goes up an octave.

"Same size as it was before, though," I say. "My wife said she didn't want to have sex with someone whose dick was green, so that kind of ended things."

"Wayne, you're going to be a lot more popular than you'd think."

As Somer makes a mess on my countertop, I brush her peelings into a grocery bag and pull a pot from the cabinet to fill with water. She tosses salt inside and dumps the potatoes inside as soon as I put it on the stove top.

"I told you to sit pretty," She says.

She doesn't pull away when I slide my hand up her back between her shoulder blades. In fact, she kisses me back as if she plotted the same move. I thought about last week every other second it seems. Somer feels soft as if I'm cradling a pillow, yet her lips push harder after a moment passes and fingernails dip into my spine.

"Those potatoes will take a while," I say.

What am I trying to lead into? That's not something I'd say. Yet I'm thinking the island is big enough for us; most importantly Somer. I ordered a couch big enough for four people to sleep on, and it's only a few yards away. My bedroom is nearby too. Amazon dropped off a package today I ordered last week: Old Spice deodorant, apple cinnamon scented candles, and a box of Trojan condoms.

"Go sit down or I'll tie you up," Somer says.

"Right," I turn around, "Maybe you can tell me why we're watching a Julia Roberts movie."

"Because *Pretty Woman* is my favorite movie," She says. "And movies are perfect for second dates."

"I'll keep an open mind," I say. "I've never seen it. There's a lot I haven't experienced, apparently."

"Same here, sugar. You said your daddy was a minister?"

"So I grew up somewhat sheltered. He didn't even let me watch the Disney Channel."

"But my entire personality is based on *The Suite Life of Zack and Cody*. You're not going to get any of my references."

"That's partially why I was an English major," I say. "I used to read a lot. That's about all I could do unless I wanted to watch *Law and Order* with Mom."

"I hate that show," Somer says. "I'd rather read too."

"Do you have a favorite book?" I ask.

"I took an English lit course last semester, and the last book we read was *Shirley* by Jane Eyre."

"You're in school?"

"I'm a music major at West Georgia."

"Whoh," I say. "I think I just came."

"Hell, I didn't know what else to do. Mama had me playing piano when I was seven."

"Last week, you said you couldn't sing," I say.

"I can't," Somer says. "But I love music. I figured everyone did, but some people will surprise you."

"I know nothing about music. It falls in the same category as Sweet Life of Zack and Miri for me."

Somer stops seasoning the steaks to squint at me. The only music I ever heard that wasn't gospel or hymns came from friends at school who would try putting their headphones on me. At work, I listened to podcasts exclusively. I still leave the radio off when I'm driving.

"Well, there's our third date right there," Somer says. "That TV of yours have apps on it? You have a sound bar underneath it. We can download Spotify and you'll want to get rid of me after about an hour."

"I will accept all forms of torture you wish to enforce upon me. Do you have any favorites?"

"*Songs From the Big Chair* by Tears for Fears," Somer says. "Then probably Led Zeppelin's first album. You heard them, right?"

"My dad mentioned if you played their music backwards, it said stuff about Satan."

"You are a grown man, Wayne. Leave your daddy at the door."

Once the steaks are cooking, Somer's attention turns to pouring butter on them with a spoon and sticking a fork into her potatoes. Given that my only superpower is cooking, she looks like she's doing everything right and we won't be eating Stouffers again tonight.

Whenever Lynn cooked, she gave me emotional whiplash when I told her it was good over and over. She never believed me. Somer sets my plate down and begins eating without interrogating me. Admittedly, this steak is better than the one I would cook. Then again, Mom always made Dad's well done.

"Did you put something on this steak that I missed?" I ask. "This can't just be salt and pepper."

"It's also rare," Somer says. "If I ever have a heart attack, I'd rather do it with a belly full of steak."

I love this version of Somer, and I'm curious who she is when the charisma, makeup, and perfectly manicured nails start to flake. Everyone gets angry, and often at stupid shit. I find most people don't get angry when it's warranted, and I wouldn't expect her to be any different. It's how we reconcile after shouting that makes the difference.

"Last week, you were watching *Breaking Bad*," Somer says. "That doesn't seem like something a minister's son would watch."

"I branched out in college. I wanna say it was Lynn's idea to watch it in the first place, but I can't remember if we were together when I first watched it."

"That your ex-wife's name?"

"Yeah," I say. "Her full name was Lynnette."

"Is that the only thing she did to corrupt you?"

"Oh, I was corrupted before I met her. I was older than her, after all. She wasn't my first girlfriend. Just the first one to stick."

"That sounds a lot spicier than what's likely to be the truth. Your corruption and all. Do you even drink?"

"No," I say. "I do not drink. I have never had a beer. I have never tried wine. My corruption was different."

"Did someone blow cocaine up your ass?"

When I applied to West Georgia, I opted to live on campus, which isn't difficult because they try to get all freshmen to spend money on a dorm room. Since I not only received the Hope Scholarship but also the College Through Christ grant, I could afford my own room. If they required me to have a roommate, I'd rather sleep in the air ducts at the library.

My intention was to sleep well and be able to lie around in my underwear without feeling shame. I still spent lots of time in the library and UCC, which originally had a Quiznos and Mexican grill that always gave me diarrhea but tasted amazing. My sophomore year, the school put in a Subway on the top floor and replaced the grill with bad sushi.

Given that I wasn't into video games at the time, and had no extracurricular bullshit other than attending weekly meetings at the Baptist Center, my free time was initially rather dull. My girlfriend, Leslie, went to Radford University, so we broke up. Kids who maintain long distance relationships with their high school fuck buddies are stupid.

Everyone needs a vice. That's likely why Dad always had his nose in the Bible instead of over a bottle. People get second jobs to fill their time so they don't need to contemplate how life is full of wasted space. Hobbies are ways to deflect thirst. I'm not talking strictly about alcohol. Humans crave primal things they can bite into like animals.

Without Leslie, I needed a new vice, and her name was Kasey. We didn't go to Waffle House at four in the morning or meet up in the library for a study group. My private room was our sanctuary. After a couple of weeks, we did go to Target together to go halfsies on a grey plastic tub for her toys.

Sexual trauma isn't a fickle concept that applies to a finite genre. Mine began with Callie, but I was unaware that I damaged myself. Firstly, I believe the amount of intercourse and masturbation I experienced as a teen destroyed a part of me I can't remedy. I last a long time. Some women, including Lynn, found this tiresome. Girls broke up with me because I couldn't orgasm with them. Each tried and ended up with a wounded ego. When I lost my erection, they tried blaming me, and I accepted that blame because it was technically true. Sex is how I explored my vice. There've been times when I came so much with Kasey and a select few that my orgasms caused me pain and my pelvic muscles needed rehab.

"If I told you," I say, "You'd run screaming."

"Are you a serial killer?" Somer asks.

"That would make me more interesting. I'm afraid I don't have anything for dessert, by the way."

"The potatoes are enough," Somer says.

I haven't seen enough Richard Gere movies to know if he actually speaks like his character or if he's purposefully affecting his speech. While Julia Roberts does a good job, I don't buy that someone who looks like her would need to hook, especially if she's pretty enough to catch a rich guy's eye. Would she be on OnlyFans if this took place in 2020? Do prostitutes even roam streets anymore?

I kinda get why Somer brought this movie, though. Aside from getting to cuddle me as we watch very conservative sex scenes, there's a love story. Even I want them to get together. Do either of them have a breeding fetish? That would make this a bit more true to life.

"Do you wonder what happens after the movie?" I ask.

"Maybe he finally overcomes his fear of heights," Somer says.

She takes the disk out of the Bluray player, and I'm watching her because I hope her next move isn't to go home. What could I say to make her stay if she does try to leave?

"I'd really rather not wait another week to see you again," I say.

"You're going to want to make sure you like me," Somer says. "Moving too fast could be bad for both of us."

"Wait, I'm supposed to the mature, restrained person here."

"See, I know that I like you, Wayne. It would've been nice to have you over for New Years. I didn't have anyone to kiss when it turned midnight. I think you know that I could've had someone with me that night, but I wanted it to be you."

Rather than tell her I would've been there, and I know I would've despite all my doubts about being in a relationship with her because of our age, I take the approach I did with Steve Sebastian. Not to play a game with her; I know she has more to say. People dig themselves into holes because they're concerned about speaking up when they really need to listen.

"And it sounds like your wife left without real time to think about things," Somer says. "I'm not jealous because I know you still love her. There's nothing wrong with someone still being in love. Don't bother me at all. But if I get too close too fast, she might come back and you'd have to drop me like a hot panhandle. It's not about you wanting me more, because that was your wife. Even if you didn't love her anymore, you might feel obligated to give her a second chance."

Making an affirmative noise, I don't want to start denying what's obviously true. I'll always love Lynn, and if Somer didn't understand that, we couldn't work. It's not like I'd constantly miss my ex-wife. Right now, I do not hope all the best for her. Eventually, Lynn is going to feel better about herself, find a new man, post their pictures together on social media, and maybe get married again. Everyone will encourage her in pursuing her happiness as if our vows meant nothing. It's not that I don't want Lynn to be happy. We were married, and no one even took a moment to consider my happiness. That should've counted too.

"There's something else you want to say," I stand up from the couch.

"We're meeting here for your sake," Somer says. "Now, I like coming here and will come back every time you ask me to. If you and I go out in public together, we're stuck together even if we break up. I will always be associated with you, and I'd never be ashamed of that, but again I don't want to be broken hearted and have you haunt me like that."

For a while, I forgot I was green. After spending a little time with Somer, I felt normal again. Thinking that diminishes my situation, though. I am normal. I don't feel about myself the way I did before I changed. Somer doesn't look at my skin as others do; she doesn't break eye contact to take in what I am.

"But you're still here," I say. "If you didn't want to date me, you wouldn't be here in the first place. If you want to take this slow, then I'll go as slow as you want. I am in only in a hurry to spend more time with you."

"Way to melt my heart, Wayne," She looks away. "So, about our next date."

"Are you busy Saturday?" I ask.

"I work," She nods. "Classes start back Monday. I gotta drive to school and back for Mondays and Wednesdays."

"Are you working Tuesday?"

"I think so, but I can come see you after."

"You need time for homework, though."

"I only have to practice my pieces," Somer says. "I took all my core classes early on."

"Smart," I say. "I wasn't smart and was still taking foreign language classes my last year."

"So, we're going to listen to my favorite albums?"

"I'll listen attentively to every note," I say.

## Chapter 12

Genevieve's secretary, Maggie, smiles as she welcomes me in, which is nicer than when she stared at me. I got a text from Genevieve that we needed to talk about my stock options as soon as possible. Microsoft isn't up or down significantly, so I'm not sure what she's talking about.

"Thanks for coming up here, Wayne," Genevieve closes the door. "Things are happening that a lot of people are either sweeping under the rug or flat out ignoring."

"Is this good or bad for me?" I ask.

"It's actually great for you. From my records, you still have a lot in savings. You haven't been dipping into them at all, so that's good, but have you heard about this virus that's spreading around in China?"

"No," I say. "I don't follow the news."

"Most people don't think it's a big deal. I got a call from one of my economics professors I keep in touch with, and he thinks this is going to spread here."

"Genevieve, unless you're carrying it right now, I don't think it's an issue for me."

"No, Wayne, it's an issue for everyone else with their money in the wrong stocks. We bought you Microsoft. If this virus spreads, office buildings like the one you worked in will shut down. EHR Interactive is going to send all of their workers home. People are going to be stuck in their homes, and that only means good things for Microsoft."

"A virus is going to do all of this?" I ask. "A virus like the flu?"

"It's called Corona," Genevieve gestures. "It's not like the flu at all. It's a lot worse. There's footage of people in China keeling over in the streets. There's so much trading and exporting going on in China, there's no way it doesn't spread."

"So you want me to buy more Microsoft stocks?" I ask.

"It will make you a very rich man," She nods. "I'm putting all my extra cash into it too."

"Okay," I say. "This is why I hired you. Why couldn't we have done this over the phone?"

There's a knock before someone opens the door. Steve Sebastian waves at Genevieve, who points at him as if answering my question.

"You should listen to her advice," Steve says.

"Are you stalking me, Steve?" I ask.

"When you're a journalist, it's called research. Can I talk to you out back?"

I follow Steve outside where we sit down and he pulls out his iPad to show me my photo in the Atlanta Journal. He seems to think this will impress me, but I don't read the paper and don't know anyone who does. At least people over the age of sixty will know who I am.

"I got a lot of emails about you," Steve says. "Your fame is going beyond an internet meme. You know what's constant in all the correspondence I get about you? Not anyone says a negative word. They're all curious about you."

"Are you going to interview my ex-wife and plumber next?" I ask.

"I'm not TMZ," Steve says. "But I am the one who gave Genevieve the tip in exchange for a meeting. That Corona thing is going to be bad if it spreads here."

"What do you want this time?"

"One of the people who contacted me was a producer at Searchlight. There's interest in a documentary about your life."

"No," I say. "If I wanted to be in a circus, I'd learn how to ride an elephant and walk a tightrope."

"It's favorable. A positive thing, Wayne. You shouldn't assume anyone is trying to exploit you."

"Thanks to you," I say, "I can't go to my local comic book store, and I might need to find a new financial advisor. You're crossing a line, Steve."

"You should know that all Coweta County property records are public," Steve says. "Someone with less than positive intentions might decide to actually stalk you."

"I have a rifle," I say. "And a pretty tall fence that would really hurt to accidentally pierce an organ on."

"It wasn't my intention to piss you off, Wayne. I apologize that I've offended you, but it was my understanding that you wanted people to accept you as you are."

"I'm no one of importance. Just a man."

Steve pulls his iPad into his lap and navigates to his emails. Having a camera crew follow me is not only an invasion of the privacy I hold dear, but the makings of a really boring movie. Then again, if Steve is such a good journalist, they might try making the film without me. That's happened before. They might dig up Lynn, Callie, Kasey, old co-workers, college professors, my parents, and Somer. Either I need to hire an attorney, or I should speak directly to this supposed producer so I can control my narrative.

"Five million," Steve puts his iPad on my knee. "I'd get a credit for my story on you, and a little part in the doc. Otherwise, it'd all be about you, man. Hell, you can afford a lawyer who'd read all the contracts for you and might even negotiate more money out of them."

"Give me a number," I say. "And stop fucking following me. I have an email address, you know."

The producer is a lady named Faith Donovan. Why did I expect this person to be Tom Cruise's character from *Tropic Thunder*? Instead, she's a forty-something with a decent IMDB page. She's even attached to the *Fire in the Engine Room* movie that's been in development hell since 2015.

We arrange a call this afternoon, so I kill time by mulling over whether or not to fire Genevieve. If she's right about this virus and Microsoft, then I might not need to fire her if she makes bank on the stocks.

"Wayne," Faith says, "Gracious, I'm happy to have you on the phone. Steve made you out to be a little bit of a stale cookie."

"I like stale cookies," I say. "Especially the soft ones."

"Well, maybe we'll see how those soft cookies crumble once we get you on the other side of the camera, huh?"

"I'm going to hang up on you, ma'am," I say.

"Apologies for the bad segue. I'd like to bounce ideas off of you, though. You came across as good humored in that interview, but a little dry. Documentaries need a narrative, a plot like any other story, you know? What do you see as your story, Wayne?"

"I'm not sure there is a story," I say. "I started changing colors, my wife left me, I lost my job, and then I sued for wrongful termination. Now I live away from everyone because I don't want attention."

"Why do the interview with Steve, then? The Associated Press put that story everywhere. Hell, I first saw it on CNN."

"Because kids are memeing me on social media," I say. "People need to know they don't have to fear me. I hope that also gives them pause about approaching me."

"I find the best way to pass your fifteen minutes is to get it over with quickly," Faith says. "We have an office in Atlanta, and I can have a contract drawn up for your attorney. We could shoot with you over a few days, and be done by the end of January."

"How can you make a movie that fast?" I ask.

"We want it on Hulu this year in order to get ahead of this Corona thing."

"What the hell is with this virus I'm suddenly hearing about?"

"It's going to be the best thing to ever happen to streaming services."

Flo meets me at the Fox offices in Atlanta, which are near the CNN Center. Getting up early on a Monday was supposed to be over in my life when I got fired. Instead, I'm clutching a Chai Latte on an elevator next to Flo, who is sipping on a sugar free Red Bull.

Faith looks like someone who believes personality is all in the eyes and how wide your lids can open. She shakes my hand like I saved her son from a caravan of thieves. Her entourage is made up of a Los Angeles attorney who resembles an outdoor sports store manager, and another producer named Jamal. As their presence begins to over-stimulate me, I look at the view of Atlanta while reminding myself that I'll never stop living in the woods.

"While Flo is going over our offer," Faith says, "I wanted to let you give us input on our plan. You're the only interview subject, which means you're carrying the film. We'll splice in photographs if you'd like to provide them from your childhood, and we can even hire an animator to help visualize your stories."

"Sounds fine," I say.

Flo nods at me and passes the contract over. I'm happy with the five million deal and don't even need that much money. Why the hell they'd spend that money on me is egregious. I suppose if people can romanticize Popcorn Sutton, I might make a decent hour-long doc for a streaming service.

"That seems almost too easy," I say.

"Hey, we're making out like bandits," Faith says. "Once we film everything, we'll wire you your money, and you can sink back into your hole."

"Couldn't you have just faxed this over?" Flo asks.

"Meeting in person lets our partners know we're serious, Mrs. Garner."

"Could you have a film crew meet me this weekend?" I ask. "I'll get your photos and you can have me all you need."

"Eager to get it over with," Faith says. "I like it. Sure, Fox has plenty of camera equipment in Georgia, though we may not have the director you'd like."

"Anyone is fine," I say. "I'm just going to talk and give every detail I can, and I'm sure your editors can pick out the good parts."

Everyone else in the room starts talking, but I'm putting all of this together as reality sets in all too soon. With this kind of money and notoriety, my life is going to only grow more bizarre. Unlike a lot of kids, I didn't envision myself as a celebrity. Dad told me to want fame and vanity is a sin, so the best way into Heaven was to remain humble, work hard in my professional life, and keep God in my heart. The scales are starting to tip in Hell's favor.

If I wasn't one eyeball away from resembling Mike Wazowski, I'd still have my job, and maybe my wife. Waking up alone, my eyes taking in the light that fills my empty bedroom, and reaching over to feel cold sheets reminds me of Lynn each morning. Sleeping by yourself is fine once in a while when you're used to sharing a bed. Constantly reliving how your spouse dumped you in each mundane activity makes me anxious to replace her.

I'll wait to tell Somer about this tomorrow, I suppose. With my extra income, I bet I can afford a piano for my house to surprise her. Getting it into my house without anyone seeing my true identity is another matter. Mom was able to arrange for furnishings without my presence. A piano might be out of her scope, but I can ask. Buying a piano on a third date, which isn't a real date at all, might come off as love bombing or incentive to fuck me.

## Chapter 13

Before I met Lynn, I briefly dated an older woman, Eve, who tried cooking in my apartment as our first date. Instead of watching her put an entire pound of hamburger meat into a frying pan without even knowing how to boil water, I offered to take over and cook for us. I have yet to disappoint someone with my spaghetti, so I do an order pickup at Walmart for Jimmy Dean sausage, a jar of Ragu, penne, frozen garlic bread, and Cherry Garcia ice cream. The bread and ice cream help with the acid reflux that inevitably occurs.

It strikes me that I could've supplanted the piano idea for buying a turntable and Somer's favorite albums. However, my sauce is bubbling and she's waiting at the gate, so I'll have to invest in an Amazon teleportation portal soon. I'm sure that's on the horizon since the drones get stolen or shot down.

This evening, Somer's gray romper and matching plaid North Face make me wonder what she'll do if she has to pee. She obviously did not wear that to work either, so she put it on specifically for us. My dick moves toward my leg wondering when I'll get to bury myself into her flesh. There's really no greater feeling than when you first get on top of a woman with meat on her bones.

"We have to hurry or my sauce might explode," I say. "I assume you don't have a tomato allergy."

"If you're making me spaghetti, you might get lucky tonight if you didn't forget the garlic bread."

"I'll make sure to bake the entire loaf."

Usually I throw in four slices and keep the other four in the freezer, but I spray my pan down with Pam and pray these carbs actually get me somewhere. I'll wait as long as Somer needs so she feels secure. There's a guy in Europe with a ten inch dick I heard about on a podcast that won't have sex with women until they've been dating for three months since so many want to skip the line to ride the ride. Unfortunately, I'm weak and haven't had sex in about six months.

"God," Somer sits at the bar. "That smell makes my toes curl."

"Then you won't mind listening to me talk for a minute while you stuff your face. Do you like butter on your noodles?"

"Boy, have you seen me? Hell yes, I want butter on my noodles."

I used to work with a woman from Italy who scoffed at such a thing. She said sometimes she would put some garlic in olive oil if she wanted to add something to her noodles, but apparently melting half a stick of butter and throwing it on bare noodles is a Southern sacrilegious act. However, I occasionally speak to someone who also puts butter in their ramen, and I consider them a true brother or sister in Christ.

"What'd you want to talk to me about?" Somer asks.

I drain the noodles and smile at her. I'm not sure how to begin. The attention I receive from this documentary will likely make me a stronger magnet for the eyes that follow me everywhere in public. That means if Somer and I ever start going off my property to meet, she's also going to get her photo taken by strangers and posted online. Maybe the five million, or the three-and-a-half million I keep after taxes, will soften the random camera flashes.

Her eyes follow the bread plate like I'm running through the kitchen naked with that man's ten inch dick. Steam rises from each spaghetti plate as if receiving God's blessing. I wait for mine to cool while Somer mixes her penne and sauce, and blows on her first mouthful. I like her eagerness.

"I've never had spaghetti like this," Somer moans. "But I'm going to gorge on this shit right now."

"While you're staining your face," I say, "I went to Atlanta for a meeting yesterday, and Fox is making a documentary about me."

Unable to speak through the noodles and sauce, Somer holds her fingers against her lips with her eyes reading shock. I'm not able to decipher if it's enthusiasm or dismay.

"I'm meeting with a film crew this weekend to knock it out," I say. "It's supposed to be on Hulu within the next few months."

"Babe, that's wild," Somer wipes her mouth. "You're really going to be famous now."

"Does this bother you at all?" I ask. "I mean, look, last week you read me the rites for this relationship. Now, I'm well aware that we're both human and flawed, but I'm not going to just fuck you and dispense with you. I'm willing to wait however long you want before we move forward, because I really like you. The thing is that you seem to be very mature for your age, which is something every older guy says to younger women, but there's always a gap. You're twenty-one, and while I'm still young, you're really still young. So when I go through with this, if we ever tell anyone about us or start going out together, then like you said you'll be tied to me forever."

Nodding along, Somer continues eating while processing what I'm telling her. I'm past the point of insecurities. She obviously likes me and doesn't have ulterior motives, and I cannot censor myself because I'm afraid to spook her. At this point, I should only be honest.

"Does my age bother you?" Somer asks.

"I think Bother is the wrong word," I say. "It gave me pause when you first came over. We haven't done anything serious, and I don't think you're wasting your best few weeks with me. But I am a homebody, and kind out of necessity at this point. I also need to get to know you better, because we're in this early phase where everything is fun and yet we're kind of strangers still."

"You're right," Somer says. "We should get to know the basics of each other."

"Before we do that," I say, "There is one more thing about this doc."

"Mmm hmm?"

"They're paying me a lot of money, and I haven't really told you how much I have to begin with. Not that it would sway you one way or the other."

"I'm in school to study piano, so money don't mean much to me."

"It will," I say. "I was an English major and thought the same way until I had to face the real world. I still think I should've studied something else."

"You're leading up to something, so just tell me."

"In my lawsuit, I received three-and-a-half million dollars, which left me with about two million after taxes," I say. "That's how I could afford to buy this entire development, put up the gate, yada yada.

But Fox offered me five million to do the doc, which will likely be closer to three after taxes. Gotta love the government."

Dipping her garlic bread in sauce, Somer's expression reads as if someone borrowed and totaled her Jetta without insurance. After wiping her mouth, she turns to me and lets her fingers slide to the back of my neck.

"I'd still be here if you were bankrupt," She says. "Money is great. I'm real excited for you, Wayne. I'm not turned on because you're rich, though. What I see in you is something kinda like me. You know, I get a lot of people looking at me. Some of them think I'm thick and they wanna fuck me. Others think I'm fat and disgusting. Women can be just as judgmental as the men. I ain't about to lie and say I didn't notice what you looked like when I first saw you, but you didn't look at me like other people. You also speak to me like your I'm equal and don't text me in broken English like every other guy. So yes, I want to get to know you, because I'm dying to get past this first chapter and get onto the next."

Most people are not this restrained. They fuck on first dates without knowing each other's last names. I think Lynn and I said *I love you* our first week together. There were other women I dated for a month that I didn't even like that much. I never loved Kasey despite spending many days and nights treating each other like cum dumpsters.

"I'll start," I say. "I'm an only child, my parents are still together, Dad is a minister and teaches, and Mom works for an industrial furniture company. She typically works with offices and hospitals, but she essentially decorated this place for me since I left all my furniture at my apartment. I'm definitely more of a mama's boy because most of the time I can't stand my father. Tell me about your family."

"Hmm," Somer chews her food. "My parents are also still together, but I'm not an only child. I am the oldest though. They had me real young. Mama was seventeen and Daddy had just enlisted, so he ended up working at Lowes when he wasn't deployed. We lived on base until about 2006, which is when my little brother, Stevie, was born. He's the total opposite of Daddy too."

"Oh really?" I ask. "Is he into fingernail polish and *Call Her Daddy*?"

"Nah. He's more into video games like *Call of Duty*, and he's not very athletic."

"I have no idea what it's like to have a sibling," I say. "I imagine it's a unique bond."

"We don't really talk much. He's aloof even from our parents."

"Your mom do anything?" I ask.

"Yeah, she got a degree a few years ago and teaches for Coweta Elementary."

"Oh, so she went to West Georgia too?" I ask.

"Yeah, she graduated in like 2014 or something."

"I was there," I say. "What was her major?"

"English with a teaching emphasis or something."

"Do I know your mom?" I ask. "What's her name?"

"Shannon Holly."

Now I can place Somer's face. I remember every single non-traditional student in my classes, and Shannon was never one to blend into the crowd. She proudly told my renaissance class that she called one of our department's professors a chauvinistic pig. There was never a period where she didn't speak about our assigned text.

"I remember her," I say. "So this made things interesting."

"Kinda hot, actually. I guess I can start calling you Daddy too."

"You don't strike me as having daddy issues," I say.

"No, but I do have CSL, and it's really bad."

"CSL?" I ask.

"Cock sucking lips."

The first album Somer puts on is *Led Zeppelin*, which definitely sounds like an album made fifty years ago. The first song, "Good Times Bad Times" has loud drums that would get a Rusty Camford kicked out of the Youth Ministry Group. Dad nearly shut down the Solid Rock Cafe youth group when he caught some boys listening to The Gorillaz. Somer mimes along to the lyrics while laying her head in my lap. The second song, "Babe I'm Gonna Leave You" strikes me as fairly poignant sounding, though there's no real chorus. Guitar still sounds like a foreign metallic noise to me.

"When I was a kid, my dad didn't really like going to the movies," I say, "So my mom took me whenever there was something we both wanted to see. That was the only time I really heard music that wasn't about God."

"What kinds of movies did y'all see?" Somer asks.

"Oh, anytime there was a Batman movie, we were there in a matinee. We saw the Star Wars prequels, the *Lord of the Rings* trilogy, *X-Men*, *Passion of the Christ* two times, even *Da Vinci Code*. For some reason, we missed all the Spiderman movies. I don't think she liked Tobey McGuire, so I had to see them on VHS."

"VHS?" Somer looks up.

"Yep, from Blockbuster," I say. "It's a dentist office now. I wonder if it still smells like that old carpet?"

"You gotta remember that Netflix was out when I was like ten," Somer says.

"How did you get into this music then?" I ask.

"Oh, Mama had my Mee Mee's CDs, and we never had iPods, so we just listened to music in the car all the time."

Oddly enough, "Shout" from this Tears for Fears album sounds older than Led Zeppelin but more polished. Any time I hear something like this, I think about Mama before I was born and what her life must've been like. Neither of my parents told me much about life before I was born. I'm not even sure how they started dating. Dad probably courted her for two years, finally popped the question, and waited two more. I don't see them as a romantic couple. They never hug or kiss one another. They don't even hold hands while watching TV.

"Your parents meet in school?" I ask.

"Actually," Somer says, "Daddy went to Central in Carroll County. They met at a football game and he used to meet her at the Steak and Shake in Newnan every Friday night, unless there was a game. They sat with each other in the bleachers for all of them."

"That sounds more romantic than my high school girlfriend," I say.

"I didn't have a boyfriend in high school," Somer says. "I still don't like guys my age."

"But you're hot," I say. "If I looked like you in high school, I would've worn the wheel off of my car."

"I told you girls can't get around here without gaining a reputation," Somer says.

"I don't remember your mom being religious or anything," I say.

"She got pregnant at seventeen, Wayne. There're a few things Jesus can't stand in the way of, and I don't care what Carrie Underwood says: A high speed train, a twelve gauge shotgun, and a man's semen. They all go fast in one direction."

"I never think much about Jesus," I say. "I always pray to God."

"I didn't go to church growing up," Somer says. "Mama liked to sleep on Sundays. Daddy don't believe in anything. That's not a problem, is it?"

"Lynn is an Atheist," I say. "I told Dad not to preach to her about it."

"You took sleeping with the enemy hard, boy."

"The more time I spend away from her, the less I remember what we really liked about each other. I acted differently with her. It was like all the other girls I dated or slept with before were practice for the real thing. That's what I said anyway. After we got married, it was good for a couple years. Then she started thinking too much. A good relationship is like a snow globe. You can look at it and appreciate the beauty, but you have to break it apart to find out what makes it so beautiful. To Lynn, it couldn't have been the water and glycerin making the snow pretty. She had to smash the glass, pour everything out, and look inside to find nothing. I understand getting depressed and feel like life is aimless. But I had to keep working to pay the bills and asking Mom for extra money when we didn't have enough left to eat with. I figured that's what a good husband does. There might've come a day when I couldn't work anymore, and Lynn would do her part. Of course, I did lose my job, and then I lost her."

Somer sits up and combs my hair with her nails before kissing my cheek. Looking at her blue eyes remedies a lot of my pain. Smelling her, hearing her breath close to me, and feeling the heat from her body extinguishes any remaining cinders from my dead marriage. I know her presence causes temporary relief. Maybe it's lust, though.

"I think I just trauma dumped all over you," I say.

"Imagine what it would be like to talk to someone who couldn't empathize with you," Somer says.

"Well, if we're being honest, this music is very strange to me. It's like you found a way to take my virginity all over again. Or like that time I went to a friend's house and a Marilyn Manson video was on TV."

"You realize that usually it's the guy who subjects the girl to new, strange things? Last time I went to a guy's place, he made me watch a movie called *Eraserhead*. I still have nightmares about that baby."

"That's a bad date movie," I say. "*Pretty Woman* was a better move."

"Thank you," Somer kisses my forehead.

By the way we get to Van Halen's *Diver Down*, I turn the TV down since Somer is snoring on my shoulder. Hopefully, her iPhone alarm is on so she's not late to class tomorrow. Rather than wake her, I put a blanket on her and turn the music off while the guitarist in this band makes dying robot sounds. I assume a four-year-old would believe it was Satan coming out of the speakers, because I almost feel the same.

Chapter 14

Thanks to *Walking Dead*, *Insatiable*, and *The Conjuring Part 69*, there are numerous spaces that cater to people who employ actors and camera crews in Coweta County. The director walks up to the Escort as soon as I park outside, and I know that's his title because it's on his baseball hat.

"Wayne?" He says.

"Gamora," I say. "Wayne had an emergency call to Xandar."

"Oh, I've seen *The Avengers*. I get that reference. I'm Ben. It's just you, me, and fourteen other people today."

I'd make an orgy joke, but then someone will hashtag me as a creep on Twitter. This is supposed to be a good PR move. The studio interior has a giant white screen, a chair, three cameras, a bunch of lights, a table full of bagels, and several people who are looking at their phones.

"Did you see the picture of me in the paper?" I ask.

"I saw the picture of you on Buzzfeed," Ben says.

"So you envisioned me taking my shirt off for the first part of the doc while you splice in my narration and shots of me looking contrite?"

"Wow. You're like a mind reader. Do you have powers?"

After standing in front of the camera, everyone's attention turns on me when I take my shirt off and walk around to show the pure green skin on my back. I even bend over and rub the crown of my head to display how my hair is thinning. The thought of investing in a couple kettlebells and a treadmill doesn't hit me until several women are clearly telepathically asking one another if my dick is green. If not for Somer, I'd get in all of the trouble to get laid.

Once I'm clothed and seated, Ben turns his hat backwards while reading from his iPhone.

"What's your name?"

"Wayne," I say. "Wayne Pallidus. I'm from Carroll County, Georgia and am currently unemployed, recently divorced, and vote blue."

A few people snicker, but Ben keeps looking down at his screen. He needs at least an hour of good content, and I might have to be the creative one here. English majors are practically Film minors, so I endured many hours of bullshit movies like *Dead Man* and *Grizzly Man*. Neither have superheroes.

"How else would you describe yourself?"

"I'm an only child. A preacher's son. An American citizen. A lover of books. My favorite book is *Invisible Man*. Am I neglecting any obvious details?"

"Describe your appearance."

"Well, I identify as a male, have brown hair, could stand to lose ten pounds, and I think my best assets are my feet."

"What would a stranger notice about you first?"

"A stranger? I think everyone notices the same thing about me first no matter how well they know me. I have green skin."

"Why do you think you're green?" Ben asks.

"I mentioned that my father is a minister. He said that this is not God punishing me for anything. My doctor said there's nothing wrong internally, but he couldn't draw my blood."

"He couldn't draw your blood?"

"Oh, my skin doesn't break anymore. You guys wanna see?"

Ben requests someone on the crew find a knife, and a grip offers his buck knife. Ally, the woman in charge of getting bagels, coffee, and whatever Ben or the talent request, gets to try cutting me since she's the best looking person on set. When I started at EHR Interactive, there was a lady in her late thirties who wore pigtails and she looked like a giant possessed doll. Fortunately for Ally, she's young and doesn't have the physique of Miss Trunchbull, so the curled strands coming from each side of her hair accentuate her inner *Lollypop Chainsaw*.

"Am I really going to cut you?" Ally asks.

"Here," I offer my arm, "I don't think there's anything too vital on the top of my arm. Cut side to side, but don't push too hard."

"How do we know that blade isn't too dull to cut you?" Ben asks.

"We'll use a razor blade if you're not satisfied with this, you sadist," I say.

As I'm holding out my left arm, Ally slides the blade too gingerly across my skin to even leave a mark. I take her wrist and press harder. There's no pain, but I feel the cold metal push deeper onto me.

"Okay, that felt legit," Ally backs away.

"We have a First Aid kit," Ben says. "Try the other side where the skin is more sensitive."

"You game, Ally?" I ask.

When I turn my arm around, Ally tries matching the slice I helped her make before. Again, there's nothing. I suppose it would be too hacky for me to pretend she actually cut me and then tell her it was alright.

"I'm done," Ally says. "There's no way that wouldn't cut me."

"Thank you, Ally," I say. "Everyone give Ally a round of applause."

She returns the knife and runs back into the darkness of caffeine and carbs. Ben doesn't look too convinced, but he claps along with the crew.

"How was that?" Ben asks.

"I haven't been penetrated by a woman in years, so it was okay," I say.

"Is that something you've tried before?"

"Pegging or cutting?"

"I think we'll cut to the next question."

After Ben asks all the possible questions about my skin, seeing myself on the internet, my parents, childhood, and living like a hermit, I'm thirsty and much of the crew is stretching or sitting on the floor. Even though it's their job, I don't want to be the reason they go to bed sore tonight.

"We can take a quick break," I look around.

"It's fine," Ben says. "I ran out of questions thirty minutes ago."

"How old are you, Ben?" I ask.

"Thirty-four," Ben says.

"Do you ever feel like you're thirty-four?"

"I don't feel much different than when I was twenty-four, I suppose."

"Is there anything you regret about your life that your age makes you feel like you missed out on?"

"I'm supposed to ask you questions."

Everyone shares a chuckle, but I'm leading into something I was thinking about the other night with Somer. Part of my fear with her is that I'll end up taking too much of her time, and she'll be twenty-eight like me and think she's wasted the best years of her life slumming it with a man who would rather stay at home with a bag of McDonalds than try snails on a fancy plate with a view of the Eiffel Tower. That's the most luxurious image I manage to conjure, but I've never desired to travel. Most young people want to see as much of the world as they can.

"I didn't get to listen to much secular music growing up," I say. "I'm sure you know who Led Zeppelin is."

"Zeppelin?" Ben says. "Sure, everyone does."

"I didn't until 2020," I say. "Never heard any of those musicians until this week. I'm seeing this woman who is younger than me, and she played me her favorite albums. I don't have a favorite album. I didn't have a CD player or iPod growing up. To see someone get such joy out of music reminded me of all the things I haven't experienced yet. When I started changing, I thought I was dying of some organ failing inside me. I spent years working at a company that didn't appreciate me, years in a marriage that failed, and years at a school that lied to me about the career opportunities for college graduates. All the time I have left in my life belongs to me, yet I feel like I've wasted so much of my potential because I tried doing everything right. I use my skin as an excuse to stay inside, locked away from everyone. I'm really the one who is afraid of what to do with my freedom now. I have no idea, and if I changed back to a typical white guy tomorrow, I'd have the same problem."

"Before we shut down," Ben says. "Is there anything you'd like to happen when people see this?"

"Sure. If people see me in public, just know that I'm trying to live my life like anyone else. I'm not a celebrity or someone special."

As I'm walking out, I do a half-hearted wave at Ally as she's cleaning up her area. She moves to follow me out the door, but I try to make it seem like I don't notice. When I'm unlocking my car, she comes over to me.

"Hey," Ally says. "I just wanted to say I think you did a good job. I disagree with what you said at the end, though."

"What's that?" I ask.

"You are special, and you're already famous. This is going to make you even more famous. No one else is like you, so even if you're a plain jane human like the rest of us, we're all going to see you as different. It might be good different or bad different, but I bet you there are people who envy what you're going through."

"Alright then," I open my door.

"Can I take a selfie with you to show my boyfriend?"

"Sure," I say. "Let's sit on my hood."

I purposefully have us sit down so I can have my hands visible in my lap. Having a photo of me with Ally out in the world might have other implications I can't address. I also form an expression somewhere between a smile and acknowledgement. Maybe I think too much?

As soon as I'm on the road, I want to call Somer. A distant part of me wants to call Lynn too. I'm aware that trying to replace Lynn with Somer isn't good for anyone, and I'm going to grieve the end of my marriage for a long time. Instead of calling either of them, I touch Genevieve's contact.

"Are you calling me on a Saturday to fire me?" She answers.

"No," I say, "I finished filming the doc a few minutes ago, and Fox is supposed to be sending me money."

"That confirmation came through yesterday," She says. "It'll be in your savings by Monday. You wanna come in then and talk about your options?"

"After sending the IRS their due," I say, "Put half in Microsoft. The other half can go in my savings."

"Yes, sir," Genevieve says. "Is there anything else you require of me?"

"Did I interrupt something?" I ask.

"I'm binge watching *Cheer* and having a glass of Riesling, so nothing important."

"Do you think I can afford a new car?"

"That would be a wise investment considering your car is older than most college freshmen."

## Chapter 15

The nearest Volvo dealership is in Marietta, and my rationale on buying a Swedish car is that a Tesla would support one of the biggest assholes to ever exist, Fords break down too quickly and cost too much to maintain, Chevys are too Dude-Bro, and anything like a Cadillac or BMW makes me come off as pretentious. No one gives a Volvo a second look, but the interiors are luxurious like you're butter melting on a cast iron skillet ready for the meat to sizzle inside your juices.

I despise the process of buying a new car. The paperwork wraps a vice around your brain while the salesman makes you their bitch for two hours. Genevieve made sure my insurance was open to covering a new vehicle and called ahead to Volvo of Marietta to let them know a green man is coming to buy a XC90, and preferably in a color that won't mind a few weeks without being washed. Black cars love to showcase every speck of shit on them.

There are only two open parking spots near the building, and as soon as I turn off my engine, someone is walking out the front to greet me. However, the man's expression turns from salesman to common spectator when he sees me in the sunlight.

"Do you need any help, sir?" He asks.

"My financial advisor called ahead," I say. "Her name is Genevieve. Someone in there spoke with her."

"I'm sorry, what now?"

"I should have an appointment with someone," I say.

"Oh, you have an appointment? Who is your appointment with?"

"Well, like I said, my financial advisor called here because I'm looking to buy a XC90."

"Hey, if you're looking to buy a car, that's where I can help you."

I follow this guy inside, who has yet to introduce himself, and there's a larger man who comes out of an office and gestures toward me.

"Hey James," He says, "This is the gentleman that lady called about."

"What lady?" James asks.

"I didn't tell you?" He asks. "I'm sorry, Mr. Pallidus. My name is Scott Johnson and I spoke to Genevieve this morning. If you don't mind sitting for a moment, I'll fill James in on your situation."

As I'm sitting in a chair that feels like it was upholstered in the Nixon administration, a woman, who I assume is a salesman, smiles at me from her desk in a more generous manner than James. She's probably fifteen years older than me, but she wears her age well.

"Alright, Mr. Pallidus," James slaps his desk. "I noticed you came in a Ford Escort, and you didn't have anyone with you."

I cross my legs and cup my chin in my hand since he didn't ask me a question, so I'm not going to give him an answer.

"So were you hoping to drive a XC90 off the lot today, or...?"

"Yep," I say.

"We'd normally consider a trade in value, even for a Ford, but I don't know if you're aware, but the Escort hasn't been in production since like 2003, so the value isn't going to be worth the space for us. We'd be happy to take it off your hands without charging you as a courtesy considering the amount of your purchase, but if you actually need some money in return for the vehicle, there is a used car lot across the road that will probably take it off your hands."

There're Karens in this world, and they're predominantly entitled white women who ask to speak to managers when things don't go their way. They block people in tight spaces, yell about insignificant bullshit, and act like everything is an injustice. Yes, there are men and people of other races who do this, but they don't have names gifted upon them by the internet. Sometimes they're called Male Karens.

In a situation like this, I could brush it off. Hell, I can afford to let them take turns hitting my Escort with a sledgehammer while I find the car with the seats that best fit my ass. However, I don't do conflict. If someone like Flo isn't around to speak for me, I'd rather leave without saying a word. But I think Somer might appreciate if I *Pretty Woman* this shit.

"Does that used lot sell Volvos?" I ask.

Now, the woman at the other desk is looking over. James doesn't seem to understand what I'm getting at, though.

"No, we actually have an agreement with them so they can't sell any Volvo vehicles," James says.

"I really wanted a Volvo," I say, "But I'll go across the street and see if they have anything I wouldn't mind driving."

As I get up to leave, Scott's chair almost falls over in his office as he gets up to follow me. I'm out the door by the time he catches up, and James walks slowly behind him.

"Mr. Pallidus," Scott says. "Mr. Pallidus?"

"Mr. Johnson," I keep walking.

"I don't think James meant to insult you," Scott says. "I can assign you a new salesman and knock off some of the price on that XC90. Genevieve told me you were buying it today and didn't need financing. I said that to James, and..."

"You can't give him to Juney," James says. "That's my commission."

"Nevermind him, Mr. Pallidus," Scott says. "That XC90 is a fine car and they're not going to have anything close to it over there."

"Do you have one in Birch Light?" I ask.

"As a matter of fact, yes," Scott says. "It has massage seats, a panoramic roof, and a media center that you can connect your phone for calls, music, whatever the hell you want."

"I'd hate to cheat James out of his commission," I say. "I think I have a compromise, though."

"Okay," Scott nods.

"Subtract the value of the Escort from his commission," I say. "I wasn't planning to pay for the extras, but I'll pay for gap coverage in full too."

"What the fuck?" James scoffs. "Scott, I'm not taking that."

"Then Juney can," Scott says. "She'll even take you on a test drive, Mr. Pallidus."

"Oh, if Juney wants the commission," I say, "I'll do the paperwork at her desk, and I'll order pizza for everyone. That sound fair?"

"Boy, you know how to make a man's day," Scott says.

"I'm vegan," James says.

"Tough shit," Scott says. "Go home, James. Come back tomorrow when you know how to speak to a customer."

The pizzas are gone by the time I sign the final paperwork and get the keys. As Juney walks me out to my new car, a man in coveralls gets in the Escort so they can move my eyesore. Likely to abandon it in the woods.

When I was in the fourth grade, my parents decided to move out of the boonies and back to the city. Part of their reasoning was wanting me to go to the city schools, but Mom thought there was something off about the house I spent half of my childhood in. The roaches and spiders were abnormally large. She once hit a long roach with the phone book, and it's organs fell out of its shell of a body as if it was dry on the inside.

Like two idiots, Mom and Dad asked me if I liked the house they settled on. Unlike our last one, this one didn't have much of a yard and everyone lived closer together. Since it was new, I first thought my new room with a skylight and all the ambiance of a walk-in closet was amazing. After the reality that I'd be leaving my home for an empty space with white walls and matching carpets, I cried while begging Mom not to make us leave.

I worry about my old car. Unfortunately, the backseat was too small to fuck around in, but I hid in there whenever I wanted to be alone. Whether Mom wanted me to listen to Dad rehearse a sermon or Lynn asked me to drive her to TJ Maxx, I had a home in that Escort.

"Excited?" Juney asks.

"New car, new house," I say. "New skin, new life. Are you going to celebrate tonight?"

"I'll buy my husband a Big Mac and let him rub my feet."

"I have never envied a man more," I say.

"Oh, you're cute with your bullshit," She says. "I heard Scott say you could take a test drive with me."

"Yeah, I said it was tempting on my customer satisfaction survey."

"That's what every woman wants to hear, Wayne. You should write a book."

Lynn was named after Loretta Lynn, and I watched *Coal Miner's Daughter* with her mom, Beverly. There's a scene when Tommy Lee Jones pulls his Jeep up to Loretta's house after she bet him that he can't ride up the mountain, and he practically commands her to jump in. I wonder if I'd get a similar response if I drove right up to the doorway at Crooks and hollered in for Somer to check out my new car? I should probably ask her to go out with me in public before embarrassing her in front of her co-workers and the old ladies buying peanut butter.

## Chapter 16

"Hey, I know we don't text for the sake of space between our dates," I type in my messages, "But can I take you out to dinner this week?"

I should hit airplane mode before the message sends. Apple really needs a five second delay and an *Are you sure you wanna send this?* option. Instead, we're all developing anxiety disorders based on proper social interaction dying in favor of watching three white dots appear on our screen whenever we have the courage to type something we'd never say out loud.

"I cordially accept your invitation," Somer texts back.

Somer's apartment is near downtown Newnan, and I imagine sharing one bathroom with two other girls is akin to fitting John Candy and Chris Farley in an Indy car together. I stepped on Lynn's various plugs for her straightener, curler, dryer, and hair vibrator many times. What happens when that number triples?

If we need a quick getaway, the restaurant is less than half-a-mile away right on the square. I remind myself of this over and over while waiting for Somer to come out. Of course, I forgot to tell her I got a new car because I wanted it to be a surprise, so I get out and wait for her while sticking out like a rotten thumb about to fall off some poor man's hand after he leaves a nail in after a construction accident.

Wearing a strapless red top and jeans tighter than snakeskin, Somer emerges from a darkened hallway as if walking to an awards ceremony for hot ass. Despite having shared some significant moments with her, my muscles tighten like I'm in high school and about to ask Peggy Sue Loudermilk to the sock hop.

"Where's your car?" Somer tilts her head.

"I'm leaning on it," I say.

"Oh, let me see what it looks inside," Somer rushes over.

"Hey, you know if seeing me get a new car gets you this excited, I can buy you one too."

"This makes my Jetta look like your Escort," Somer rubs the dashboard.

"I was only half-joking," I say.

"I'm not going to let you buy me anything but dinner tonight, mister."

The Frame Shop is a typical aesthetically based restaurant with bare brick walls, dim lighting, tieless waiters in black shirts, and a fountain. People used to put wallpaper and tiled flooring in their establishments, or at least some paint and tablecloths. Someone figured out they could trick us all into thinking rustic is in vogue.

A maître d' looks up from what looks like Dad's pulpit stand and his eyes turn to silver dollars. Since Somer reminds me of strawberry ice cream after running around on the playground on a humid day, I'm not sure if this guy likes her or me more.

"Hi," He swallows.

"Hey," Somer waves.

"Do you have a reservation?"

"Pallidus," I say. "Seven o'clock."

He grabs two menus without taking his eyes off me and leads us to a booth. I'm sure the waiter will be just as delighted to see us. Not even a second after we're seated, I see a guy taking our picture on his phone from across the room. Hopefully, Somer doesn't get her contact prescription updated and keeps thinking I'm handsome. Otherwise, the inevitable reaction to us in public might turn her off of me.

"How did filming go?" Somer asks.

"I wanted to call you as soon as it was over," I say.

"And why didn't you?"

"Hell, I don't know," I say. "I spent a few hours in front of a camera acting like a circus animal. I let a woman try cutting me, I took my shirt off, and I got to thinking about you. Listening to that music with you made me realize I'm missing a lot in my life."

"There's a lot of music, so I hope you're prepared for more existential thoughts."

"I have an uncle. He's my great uncle, so he's my mother's uncle too. He was in the service and this was back in the fifties. My grandmother introduced him to this girl studying to be a nurse, and he was due back for deployment soon. They went on three dates before he proposed to her. They're still together. That's insane, isn't it?"

"How many women did he date before her, though?" Somer asks. "I bet there wasn't much selection."

"He's the only uncle to remain faithful to his wife or not end up divorced. Three dates. But I've been married and it's constant work. You never stop dating each other or you're occupying the same space until you drift apart."

"You're kind of a serious guy, Wayne," Somer says.

Somer orders the lamb and potatoes, which comes with the bone still in the meat. I get shrimp and grits, which I have to add salt to. Of course, neither of us are full after finishing. The bill is almost eighty bucks without the tip.

"Do you wanna walk around the square?" I ask.

"Why don't we go dancin' and order double cheeseburgers once we're starving again in an hour?"

"Where can we dance around here?"

Turns out, Newnan doesn't have a honky tonk bar where people line dance while scuffing their boots on the floor. Instead, we end up in the Big Lots parking lot as Somer's iPhone plays Dwight Yoakum in the Volvo with all the doors open. Some acoustic song about a guy sad when a woman leaves him. Probably ran over his dog and shit in his hat too.

I suppose I don't need to be much of a dancer when Somer leads the beat. Being this close to her looking so good makes my eyes water.

"How much do you like me?" Somer asks.

"More the than a pig likes slop," I say.

"Whoh, listen to the poetry coming from your lips."

"I don't reckon you like me as much as I do you," I pinch her butt.

"Oh, I like you fine. My go to analogy wouldn't be a pig loving slop, though."

"Why'd you pick this song, by the way?" I ask. "It's kinda sad."

"I had it stuck in my head all day and wanted an excuse to slow dance with you."

Since I didn't have a chance last time, I put my thumb on her chin to tilt her head back and kiss Somer. Someone oughta take a picture of this. Since we're in public, I have to refrain from letting my hands slide to her butt, but I'm a diabetic with low blood sugar sitting in front of a fresh slice of cake.

"Now what do you think your old lady would think of that?" Somer presses her forehead to me.

My heart lets its presence known at the thought of Lynn seeing the photo of me out with another woman only a few weeks after our divorce. She left me, so why do I need to feel guilty for trying to move on? I suppose people would say it's in poor taste, but Lynn really left me emotionally before we broke up. I might as well have shared a bed with Dad. I'm sure Lynn saw the meme of me and thanked herself for ending things. What am embarrassing freak I am to her; the woman I pledged my life to.

"I can't tell if your squeezing me is a good thing or a bad thing," Somer says.

"Oh," I loosen my grip.

If I get too deep into these thoughts, I'll end up crying and embarrassing another woman. Though the notion is that my brain is dealing with everything changing in my life, I don't feel worthy of Somer's presence because I am an abomination to humanity. But this change was out of my control. God and my doctor never gave me an explanation as to why.

"What you thinking about?" Somer asks.

"Whether I want Krystal or Taco Bell," I say.

"Oh fuck," Somer leans back. "Don't tease me, daddy."

"I'm hungry enough to have a little of each."

"Now I like you more than a beetle loves shit."

"Think I could persuade you to come to my place to eat again?"

"As if I'd turn down the offer."

While I was thinking we'd get a few burgers and Dorito tacos, we end up with a case of Krystals, a Nachos Bell Grande, two chicken chalupas, and a large Baha Blast we split in the car on the way home. Somehow the food remains intact by the time we're in my driveway. I have an urge to go down on Somer and fuck her in the car right now, but I'm also starving.

The leftovers go into the fridge, and we lie on the couch recovering from our food orgy. I guess this makes date number four another one without us taking a trip to Pound Town. There's an admirable quality to that. Somer talks a big game, but she might have limited experience and want to wait for personal reasons. Sex is a very small portion of our lives, and people act like it's this wonderful thing like we have rollercoasters hidden away in our bedrooms. Admittedly, I know I wouldn't have any issue getting off with her because she's my body type and I often lose myself in daydreams wondering what our first time will be like. I got to a point in my marriage when I didn't care that Lynn stopped wanting to have sex. She was depressed, but I'd had enough for one lifetime before we even met. I wish my brain had less thoughts about sex and more about the substantial aspects of life. Perhaps there's no such thing.

"What's on your docket for tomorrow?" I ask.

"What is today?" Somer asks.

"Wednesday," I say.

"I think I have tomorrow off."

"You want to see a movie?" I ask.

"There's not out I really want to see," Somer says. "I already saw *Star Wars* twice."

"Yeah, I went with my mom to see that when it came out," I say.

"You a mama's boy?" Somer pokes me in the stomach.

"Dad doesn't do fun things," I say. "He's too busy with Jesus and grading papers."

"Does he think people are going to Hell if they have premarital sex?" Somer asks.

"Honestly, I don't know," I say. "He and Mom definitely did it before they got married, though."

"He ever tell you you're going to Hell?"

"Not directly. He usually says doing certain things will result in going to Hell, but I always counter that I don't believe Hell exists. We have no evidence Heaven or Hell exist. There could be an afterlife where everyone goes to the same place and nothing happens."

"There's a Talking Heads song about that," Somer says. "If God is love, then I don't believe there can be any sin when your heart wants something."

"I suppose there is a difference between being horny and desiring something on an emotional level."

I cock an eyebrow and turn to face Somer with my arm pulling her to me. Instead of her lips, I move for her jaw and make my way down to her neck. As much as I love talking about our mortality, I want to at least taste her more. It's the pheromones we're all after.

"Sir," Somer says.

"Alright, I can settle down," I say.

"I already want to fuck you bad enough," She says.

"Well, I don't want you to leave me tonight," I say.

"Good, because we have a lot left to learn about each other."

Chapter 17

My Messenger app lights up on my phone as I'm one mile into my treadmill run. Wilson Mitchell sent me something, but we're not Facebook friends, and I haven't logged onto my actual account since October.

"EHR is sending all of us home," He texts. "We're working remote for two weeks. There's a chance it'll be longer, though."

Rather than respond, I turn my phone around and keep running. Trump declared a National Emergency today, which lines up with Genevieve's predictions. Somer and I went to Walmart last night out of curiosity, and most of the shelves were clear and the toilet paper was gone. I should've invested in Charmin.

All my news comes second hand through Somer or Genevieve. Both of them express paranoid thoughts about how this is going to isolate everyone. If the world goes on lockdown, people aren't used to being by themselves. They don't know how to be bored. It's only two weeks, though.

My doc is supposed to be on Hulu on the nineteenth, so everyone's about to think of me as their close friend while I don't know any of them. Part of me hopes it flops, but the attention might lead to more positive interactions. I doubt people will stop taking my picture when I go out for a while. People gawk at Somer while she's checking customers out. That would bother me, but she waves and smiles as if they're not secretly judging her for letting the green man defile her. That hasn't happened yet either.

From my rear windows, I don't see any neighbors; only trees that obscure any amount of distance. While I don't hope this virus hurts anyone, the forced isolation might give people the perspective I faced when I moved here to be away from them. In an apartment or neighborhood like my parents live in, everyone lives close together yet pretend there's not another person on the other side of their walls. Even noiseless headphones can't maintain that illusion sometimes.

  In a sense, I didn't choose to remove myself from society. Lynn pushed me through that door. EHR Interactive and all the people I thought were my friends threw cold water in my face with the realization that none of them cared whether I moved to China or drowned in a mud puddle. They all wanted me gone somehow. I'm not under the illusion that I'm special this way. Most people would rather others not infringe on their face, breathe the same air, or make them wait in line for coffee. When they get a chance to unify against one person, they'd do the same to anyone in their group if it meant making the freeway move a little faster.

  "Good luck," I text Wilson back.

  I was one less salary EHR Interactive had to pay, so of course they let me go. They invested in a new India branch before I left, and they assured everyone their jobs were safe. BPOs from companies like Polaris get a lot of the grunt work done through calling insurance companies who are also outsourced to India, but there's a liability involved. What if the company had all their employees overseas working for less with the same training? By May, I bet the first round of layoffs will make everyone who survived think their jobs are secure. There'll be another round until the only ones left are working in a call center answering angry patient calls about getting a fifteen dollar bill because United Healthcare doesn't cover their entire claim.

Soon, I hope to park my car in front of the empty EHR Interactive building, see a For Sale sign somewhere, and gaze at the place that shelled us all during the days we did too much work for too little money. While Microsoft and Amazon will get sucked off by the new economy that'll develop, these smaller corporations that dreamt of making their CEOs millions of dollars will end up losing their customer base altogether.

Mom is calling me, so I stop the treadmill and towel off my forehead.

"Hey," She says too loudly.

"Mom," I say.

"What are you doing?"

"Running," I say.

"Your dad is cancelling Sunday and Wednesday services for the next two weeks."

"So I have another excuse not to go to church."

"West Georgia has moved all classes online too, so he's going to hunker down with me for a while. Do you need anything?"

"Mom, do you need anything?" I ask. "I'm the millionaire."

"No," Mom laughs. "We still have plenty of toilet paper from when we got groceries last week."

"Did you stock up on meat?" I ask.

"No. Why?"

"You'll want to have plenty of chicken and beef, and canned stuff."

"You know we don't eat anything out of a can."

"Oh yeah, I forgot we're not a normal family," I say. "Listen, I'm not sure what's going to happen, but I don't think you guys should go out at all unless you really need something."

"We don't wanna go anywhere, Wayne."

"You can't come visit me either. Think you'll be okay with that?"

"It'll be okay for a couple of weeks."

"Mom, this isn't going away in two weeks."

"Well, if your dad needs to help someone, you know he's going to ignore all the warnings."

"A couple things I need to tell you," I say. "Can you listen for a minute?"

"Yeah."

"There's a documentary coming out about me on the nineteenth," I say.

"Flo told us about that," Mom says.

"I talk about you two on it," I say.

"I'm not too worried about that because I know we didn't traumatize you too badly."

"I'm also seeing someone," I say.

"Oh?"

"I mention her in the documentary. Not by name."

"Wait," Mom says. "Didn't you make that in early January?"

"Yes," I say.

"You were dating someone right after your divorce? Wayne!"

"We're still just holding hands if that makes you feel better."

"Has Lynn talked to you?"

"Why would she?"

"I think she blocked me on Facebook. Do you think she's okay?"

"She probably found someone who wants to spend all their money and go into debt while they live their best life traveling to places they can't afford to be."

"Me thinks thou doth hold much animosity."

"I love you," I say. "I gotta take a shower."

My last date with Somer, which ended with our excursion to Walmart as we gazed upon the beginning of the end, was a slight recreation of our first night together. She brought over two Stouffers Salisbury Steak dinners, wore the same clothes, and ended up kissing me in her Jetta before I had to go home.

This so-called lust has lasted me two-and-a-half months. I'm beginning to believe it's love. Somer's a brilliant schemer the way she makes me court her and limits how much we touch. I've had sex with women whose faces I forgot a week later. The delayed gratification doesn't make my heart grow fonder, but I'm likely respecting her more because she sets boundaries. I imagine I'd still love and respect her if she'd let me get her off, though.

Mom bringing Lynn up only reminded me that I'm forgetting her. My wife's face blurs in my mind and my happier memories exclude her. Conversations I had with her parents even seem to erase her presence. The person I would've died for discarding me like a used tampon caused me enough grief. She doesn't deserve to linger in me.

I suppose the tragedy of life is knowing people who live on without you. They're still alive, so you're waiting for them to either reach out or die. Once they were so close to you, and they either move away, fade out of your stratosphere, or simply stop talking. Before social media let you stalk anyone from a distance, I bet it drove them insane to wonder where their friends and lovers were.

I figure Mom is calling me back, but it's Somer. There must be a sinkhole in the middle of town sucking everyone to Hell, because we rarely talk on the phone.

"Wayne, the world is falling apart," She says.

"What's up?"

"First thing, people have raided the store and we may have a delay in getting stock again. My manager says I have to come in this weekend to help unload any trucks that might come in."

"What's the second thing?" I ask.

"Terri and Shayna are going home," Somer says. "They're breaking our lease agreement and moving back in with their parents. I'm fucked."

"How much is left in your lease?" I ask.

"We all signed an agreement that says if one of us leaves, the others have to pay their share until we find a roommate. Now I have no roommates. They called me while I was on my lunch break and they're already moving out."

"But how much would you owe?" I ask.

"Our total lease agreement is for $11,388, and we have three months left before renewal."

"I'll pay the rest," I say. "It's nothing for me."

"I don't know if I can let you, Wayne."

"Move in with me."

"What?"

"You can make the upstairs your own space," I say. "We can get you a piano, vanity for your make up, racks for your clothes, and anything you want."

"I mean, I wanted to move in with you for a while, but I had this lease."

"You don't anymore," I say. "I'll take care of it. And you don't need to go into work tomorrow either."

"Really?" Her tone brightens.

"I think we should talk more in person," I say. "I can be over at your place to help get your stuff in an hour."

"Wait. What do we need to talk about? I got enough stress from everything going on."

"It's nothing serious."

"Tell me," Somer says.

"It's something I should say to your face."

"What?"

"Obviously, it's nothing bad if you're moving in with me."

"Okay. I'll see you in an hour."

The apartment complex doesn't even have the hum of AC units or dented beer cans scraping against the asphalt in the wind. When I met Somer here two weeks ago, I couldn't find a parking space. Now there are only three cars aside from her Jetta.

Somer lets me in and immediately shuts the door while standing against the metal frame as if keeping out a horde of zombies.

"What did you need to tell me?" She asks.

"Oh, I probably shouldn't have said anything," I say.

"Say it."

"It might be too soon."

"Are you about to propose to me or ask for money?" She laughs.

"Wow," I say. "I guess I need to return this ring."

"What then?"

"It seems kind of childish, and soon."

"Soon?" Somer says. "Are you pregnant?"

"I'm in love with you, okay? Have you started packing yet?"

"Uh, no, no," Somer grabs my arm. "What did you say?"

"I asked if you started packing yet."

"Wayne."

"I'm in love with you. I love you. I think about you all the fucking time. And frankly, I'm tired of this cute shit. I want us to be together, and I want to fuck you."

"Okay then," Somer says. "And no, I haven't started packing. I just got home a minute ago."

"Somer."

"Of course I love you too, Wayne. Can we get me out of here before the abandonment sets in?"

"Yes, ma'am."

Nothing ever matches the excitement of someone moving in with you. Sure, it might be sudden, but you have to take the chance. Instead of only seeing each other when it's convenient, you're ass-to-ass in the same bed. Somer and I haven't even slept together; never mind sex. She's a college student, so her belongings fit in a few boxes, and the rest can stay for the landlord to dispense with. When someone's whole life can fit in my Volvo, they were never home to begin with.

Somer looks around the house as if she's inside for the first time. With her possessions at her feet, she kicks off her Converse sneakers and collapses on me.

"We should've done this the first night I came here," She says.

"That would've fizzled real quick," I say.

"Take my clothes upstairs, please. I'll move my other stuff in their new places."

By the time I get the three boxes upstairs, I lie down on the floor to catch my breath. I'm twenty-eight and starting over again with a twenty-one year old college student who is about to finish her degree in music. If she sticks with me, she'll never want for anything. Of course, that's wishful thinking, because I bored Lynn to death. I might end up doing the same thing. She's different, and so am I. Besides, when this Corona thing is over, I'll go anywhere Somer wants and be able to put in the work I couldn't when I was in a cubicle.

"Wayne?" Somer calls.

"I'm still up here," I say.

"Can you show me where to put something?"

I follow her voice to my bedroom and I think she's done unpacking since Somer is only wearing a matching black bra and thong. Considering I haven't seen any of her body before now, I feel like I'm watching porn for the first time on a dial up modem. Picking up her phone from the bed, she hands it to me.

"Put our phones in the kitchen and come back," She says.

When I return, Somer shuts and locks the door. It's unnecessary since we're alone, but I know how power moves work. Instead of making my move, I stand there letting her plot unravel. How long has she planned this? Perhaps months of teasing with a kiss or two during our evenings together were building up to this moment or genuine tests of our discipline?

"You say that you love me," Somer leans in. "Do you feel shame about anything?"

"Yeah, I'm green," I say.

"No," She rubs her palm against my cheek. "You're beautiful. I've never seen someone like you in my life, and I would bet my soul that you haven't looked forward to this as much as I have."

I'm almost scared. Her tone suggests I'm about to have candle wax poured on my nipples and a pentagram will appear over the bed. She walks to the footboard and sits against the railing as if displaying an offering. There's a ritualistic vibe as if we're finally fulfilling a prophesy.

"Do you want to see the rest of me?" She asks.

"What do I have to do?"

"Take all of your clothes off. I want to see you too."

"But you don't have all your clothes off."

"I'll take them off after I get to see you."

At this point, I shouldn't care what her motives are. She's moved in with me and I've been wanting her too long. I've never felt shame in taking my shirt off, but the pants make me feel a bit more vulnerable when they drop and I'm in my socks and boxers. No man looks sexy reaching down to take off his argyle prints. Had I known, I would've worn my black pair of boxer briefs instead of floating peaches. American Eagle's sense of humor isn't appropriate for any occasion. When I put my thumbs on the elastic waist band, Somer nods, but not in approval. It's a command.

Instinctively, I want to cup my cock and balls as if I'm shielding them from the hot water in the bath. Confidence only runs so far. I'm young, but I'm not so young that I have a constant erection. I'm hoping she realizes my size isn't at its prime, especially when someone is seeing me nude in this skin for the first time. George Costanza's voice echoes in the background, though I'm the only one who hears him. To be fair, I was harder when I saw Somer in her underwear and thought she was about to fuck me to death. Then she started throwing out commands and I got self-conscious. No one wants their first time together to be disappointing.

"Get under the covers," Somer says.

I unclench some when I get warmth back around Mick, Keith, and Charlie. Once I'm able to look at her again, I'm getting hard as Somer stands at the foot of the bed, turning around to face away, and slides her thong down. I think she's a mind reader, because that's the first thing I wanted to see. It would be weird if I asked to see her asshole, right? She waits to take her bra off until she's on the other side getting in bed with me.

When she gets on top of me, the feeling of her weight against me with our skin finally touching is already better than most sex I had in college. Anticipating this for so long, Somer rubs both hands up from my chest to my shoulders and back down to my ribs as if indulging in the textures of fresh leather. As she leans into me, I think she's about to kiss me, but her hand wraps around my dick, fingers circulating down to the base, and there's a hard pinch on my neck that confuses me between the pain and intensity growing below.

"I like that your skin is unbreakable," She takes her teeth out of my neck. "I just wanted to taste you. Every time I look at you, I wish I could eat you up."

"Just don't bite me below the waist," I say.

"Mmm nnn," She kisses along my neckline. "I didn't want it to hurt. I'll be good now."

I'm anticipating her putting my head in her mouth when she holds me steady in her hand, but Somer licks the precum off in one lash before letting her breasts envelope around me.

"Fuck," I say.

"Not yet," She says. "Just a taste."

"I want to taste you too," I say.

Relinquishing my cock, Somer lies next to me and pins her knees together so I can climb on top before spreading her legs with her feet rubbing against my calves as I press my face into her chest. I can't help being boyish when I finally get to feel her breasts against my cheeks and in my hands. After inhaling her scent, I use the tips of my thumbs to rub her nipples before taking the left one into my mouth, which makes her feet dig into my calves. Her body clenches as I kiss downward to her waist.

"Unlike you," I say, "I only bite where it's fleshy."

Somer takes in a sharp breath when my teeth press into her right inner thigh. She tastes good. I have a tendency to lose myself when I eat a woman out, though. Sometimes I lose my erection focusing in on the right balance of pressure, sucking, whether or not to slide in my fingers, and maintaining the same pace and position as they move their pelvis so I keep hitting the spot they're clamoring for. I could always get hard again when I go back to sucking their tits, or considerate women like Kasey would take their turn going down on me.

With the right foreplay, I don't last as long, but my mind often distracts me and I end up having to focus on pumping while thinking of every porn I've ever gotten off to. That's usually when I'm forced to have sex in the dark and can't see who I'm fucking. Men are visual creatures, so having nothing to look at can be a disadvantage.

You're supposed to talk about important things like birth control and condoms before getting to the point of wondering if you should pull out. I also end up switching positions a few times before I'm there. I'm still on top and trying to hold off with Somer putting me in tighter with her legs wrapping around me.

"Are you going to cum?" She asks.

I'm trying not to hold my breath as I focus on finishing, so I let out a noise while nodding my forehead against Somer's shoulder. Now is point where I need to pull out, but she's keeping me inside.

"Keep going."

Chapter 18

An American philosopher, who I think goes by the name Segura, once said that cumming inside of a woman for the first time is akin to having listened to music with cheap earbuds for years and finally hearing your favorite song in stereo.

Throughout my teenage years with Callie and Leslie, I either wore a condom or pulled out when we got caught up in the moment. There's a special trauma men experience related to their initial sexual years. Yes, I'm aware that women face a whole array of trauma in their lives from birth until death. Men merely face some of the same obstacles from a different perspective. If a man and woman end up in a car wreck together where the driver in the other car dies or a similar tragedy occurs, these two people will experience that trauma in their own unique way.

It's a common story for a boy to have sex for the first time and convince himself that he got the girl pregnant. This thought process can induce panic attacks, temporary eating disorders, depression, mania, etc. I am not unique in thinking my sperm somehow broke through a perfectly intact condom.

I never minded condoms and still think they feel good, but unprotected sex is a much different experience. For one thing, a man doesn't have to worry about a condom slipping off inside the woman. I ran to the bathroom with more than one partner to pry a latex sheath out of them.

Each of these terrible aspects involving ruining your life through pregnancy and condoms being finicky at best doesn't deter us from having sex again. After all, we're all a bunch of animals trying to procreate.

I have also paid the fifty bucks for Plan B. I didn't have to with Kasey because she had an implant that somehow killed all my sperm. I'm not a doctor or scientist, so I'll assume it worked and she didn't hide a pregnancy from me.

However, I had a lot of apprehension with Lynn when we tried having a baby. Even with Kasey, I pulled out or wore a condom. Everyone tells you horror stories about people who take every precaution and still end up with a baby. So, now I was shooting off fully loaded rounds with no goalie.

Then I discovered the dumbest concept about sex I have ever heard: the breeding kink. Most of us have a biological need to procreate. That's why calling it a kink is kinda redundant. However, some of the appeal originates with the fear we experienced as teenagers. There's also the common tale that women like to trap men by getting pregnant. I'm not saying it doesn't happen, but I've never met a woman who would put her body through the pain of bearing a child for some guy who is only halfway interested in her. However, there are definitely porn videos where the male performer tries pulling out, and he acts totally dumbfounded and panicked when the woman wraps her legs around him or won't get off. Those videos fell out of vogue because they're mildly rapey. If a man did that to a woman, it would be sexual assault.

There's a lot to the statement "Cum inside me" that thrills and repels us. Feeling like we're doing something in the moment that could fuck up everything later is hot. If sex was an intellectual activity and not the exchange of fluids Hollywood tries to erase from their films, we wouldn't have any babies.

Yesterday afternoon, Somer and I finally hopped the train to Pound Town. The experience was like a surprise party where I got everything I added to my Amazon Wishlist. Well, there are other things I want to do with her, and it's difficult to bring up the topic of me letting my mouth touch other places. The only place I haven't licked on a woman before is inside her eyeball. I don't think the scalp counts, but there might be a whole group of people into eating hair that I'm unaware of.

Afterward, Somer walked to the bathroom with my t-shirt between her legs. I used to keep a towel on my bedside table when I lived with Lynn. We always had to time me pulling out just right so it wouldn't drip out on the sheets. I stayed in bed until Somer returned, and seeing her naked again made it difficult for my erection to stay down.

I know that my physical attraction to Somer feels like I'm with the woman where God finally got it right, but I said the same about Lynn. The difference is her personality and wit. As I'm looking at her asleep next to me, I'm seeing her for the first time without make up, perfect hair, and an outfit that accentuates her figure. Instead, I see a baby face with light freckles. She looks even younger.

Now she's living with me, and I almost feel like her guardian. I do want to take care of her, and I know there's going to be a honeymoon period where we fuck, cuddle, and walk around in our underwear a lot. The time everyone wishes they could perpetuate but inevitably grow comfortable with one another to the point that they have sex once a month if they're lucky.

My cynicism isn't directed at Somer so much as my previous experiences. I'm a young divorcee and consider people like my uncle who married someone after three dates while remaining married. Not every long marriage is a miserable experience people like to be catty about. I haven't even considered marrying again. Despite loving Somer, I know better than to get married soon after a divorce. It looks tacky and is usually a bad move.

Yesterday was exciting because so much happened at once. Today is different no matter our expectations. Somer's blue eyes looking at me as she pulls me to her without speaking is a treasure, though. Yes, the presentation and masks we wear early in a relationship are nice for a while. Seeing one another in vulnerable states is what makes or breaks the bond.

"Ahh shit," Somer whispers. "One of us has to make breakfast."

"I put bacon in the fridge last night," I say. "Do you want eggs?"

"I'll take them however you make them. Ain't I lucky to have such a gentleman making me breakfast?"

# Chapter 19

I considered setting an alarm or staying up to watch the doc. Instead, I wake up at nine with Somer asleep on top of me. My breathing wakes her up, and she crawls over me instead of turning over and going back to sleep.

"Do you want me to heat up our leftovers?" She asks.

"Yeah, I'll get the TV ready," I say.

With a quesadilla and rice covered in queso on my lap, we start the movie, and the fork shakes in my hand while making a scraping noise against the plate.

"We could eat and then watch it," Somer says.

"I'm fine," I say.

She's wanted to watch this since I told her about it. The opening shot is a cold open of me taking my shirt off in front of the camera. Photos of me before the change flashes on the screen as background music starts playing. There's a close up of me sitting and apparently contemplating something, though I can't remember what. Just as I open my mouth to speak, the title card appears: *Going Green*. Instead of the movie beginning with my voice, I hear Lynn speaking.

"What the fuck?" I hear myself say.

Somer hasn't seen Lynn before. She never even asked me to see a picture of her. Now, my ex-wife looks at both of us through the screen. I thought the contract stipulated that I was the only one to appear in the film, but I'm not the one who was supposed to read the contract anyway. I trusted Flo to hold my best interests. Maybe Fox figured the risk was worth the reward.

"Why'd you leave your husband?" Ben's voice asks off camera.

"I bet he said it was because of his skin," Lynn says.

"That was one of the reasons."

"I'd been thinking of going off on my own for a while," Lynn says. "Wayne wasn't an asshole or anything. He took care of me, but I don't think he ever had a sense of adventure. When we got married, I thought I was ready to be a wife. I just didn't realize all that entailed."

Then I reappear on the screen.

"Lynn was my best friend," My image says. "Then she was my only friend. When that friendship died, I'm not really sure."

Somer pauses the movie and takes the plate from me. Seeing Lynn and hearing her say what my memory was trying to bury makes me wonder if I was wrong to marry her in the first place. Sometimes giving the person you love everything isn't what they wanted.

"She's not supposed to be in this, is she?" Somer asks.

"It supposed to be me," I say. "My story."

"Do you wanna quit watching?"

"Press play."

When the screen shows Ally trying to cut me, Somer leans in while biting her lip. Her nails leave red marks on the back of her neck. Lynn shows back up on the screen as soon as Ally walks off screen.

"I don't remember how we met," Lynn says. "I think my memory clicks back on around the time he finished school and started working at EHR Interactive."

Then I reappear to say, "We met at a local dive that was open until four in the morning, and I was waiting on wings when she walked in with her friend."

"I told him to quit a few times," Lynn says. "I didn't care if we had to borrow money from his Mom and Dad, you know? That job didn't pay him enough to stress about someone else's money. They gave him a few trophies that he had to give back, and his boss would tell him he was one of the best claims analysts there, but the next day she would get onto him for something stupid. He never showed up late, took unnecessary overtime, or used his phone at his desk. And he'd come home to cook and clean. I used to try making Hamburger Helper or tacos, but I gave up. Like, I didn't understand why we couldn't do anything. Why I couldn't do anything. Why everything have to revolve around money and the money we didn't have."

Twitter is probably talking about how wild it is that the producers brought my ex-wife in on this, and there'll be two factions: Those who say she's a big mouthed bitch who abandoned her husband while violating our vows, and the others will say her story deserves to be heard because she couldn't help not getting what she needed from our relationship. I partially agree with both, though I don't believe in calling her names. The only reason my perspective is on this screen is because people in a board room thought my skin would make them a profit during the pandemic. Everyone's stuck at home, so why not exploit the freak?

At no point have I wished suffering on Lynn. Her taking money to talk to a camera without my knowledge was to her benefit, and I hope they gave her enough so that she can take care of herself. I never put in an effort for reconciliation or fighting the divorce because I love her, but I obviously didn't know what was in her best interest.

"I feel bad for her," Somer says. "Ain't nothing like dissatisfaction."

"I'm sorry?" I say.

"You read. Haven't you heard of King Midas? Everything he touched turned to gold and it was never enough until he ruined everything in his life."

"Who is Midas in this scenario?" I ask.

"She is," Somer slaps my knee. "Duh. She got to stay at home and work on finding herself, her husband worked his ass off, she didn't miss any meals, and the most important thing she took for granted was you. Listen, I know I might be biased, but I wouldn't leave my husband if he suddenly turned green, blue, purple, or technicolor like an oil spill."

"I love you too," I say.

"I wasn't talking about you," Somer says. "I was talking about my metaphorical husband. You are not my husband, sugar foot."

As soon as the credits appear, Somer exits out of Hulu and sits on my lap. The psychological wonders of a big ass. Now would be a great time for me to relapse into my sex addiction and end back up in the urologist's office for a dry prostate and strained pelvic floor.

"Are you mad?" Somer asks.

"No," I say. "Not at Lynn, anyway."

"Okay, honey. Would it make you feel better if I let you make me lunch?"

"Lunch?" I say. "We just ate."

"An hour ago, and it didn't fill me. Could you make me ramen?"

Somer kisses my neck.

"Alright," I say.

Then she gets right behind my ear and whispers.

"And maybe a grilled cheese?"

"When you're done eating, can I put my face in your ass while you take a shower?" I ask.

"Maybe after it digests and I take some probiotics for the gas."

Good stovetop ramen and grilled cheese sandwiches require the same ingredient to make them go from palatable to impressive: butter. Apparently, breaking ramen apart in the bag before cooking it is a Southern thing, but it makes sense. Kroger carries Sapporo, which tastes more savory than the salty Maruchan or Top Ramen. Adding salted butter after draining out the excess water conforms to the junk food sensibility better than adding an egg while cooking, which I never cared for.

I never met a person who stopped cooking something because of a break up. Maybe they'll stop eating a specific dish, but I only associate my food with good times. And it's true that I am packaging away my memories of Lynn with weak strands of scotch tape, but I don't know her anymore. She didn't give me an opportunity to get to know who she wanted to be. People take photos of themselves in a mask of makeup, expensive clothes, and holding vapid drinks in overcrowded clubs, but there's no real pleasure in that world.

Society and internet culture like to scold everyone for what they eat too. This hasn't put Frito Lay, McDonalds, or Nabisco out of business, though. Documentaries about diets and the evils of bad food come out every other day. Unfortunately, I don't buy that people who deprive themselves are happier. My happiest memories in any relationship aren't based around sex or going into debt doing things we couldn't afford. The real happiness comes from when we're not wearing our shields, trying to portray ourselves as more than human, or planning for a future that never pans out. Sitting on the couch in our underwear with the TV on while eating the food we shouldn't have makes the time spent working or whatever God never intended for humans to endure worth it.

"At least you won't get mobbed for this," Somer says between bites. "No one is going to be out."

"It's weird to think about millions of people finding out I exist but we're all in our own worlds right now."

"I bet Lynn is getting her inbox blown up, though. All the people who can't find you on social media are going to take it out on her."

"That's another reason I wanted it just to be me," I say. "I didn't want my parents or random people I worked with talking about me. Nothing positive can come out of strangers harassing you."

"How tough do you think your skin really is?" Somer asks.

"Are we talking about my actual skin?"

"Yeah, like when I bite you, I never draw blood."

"You need to contain yourself a little better."

"I just like you, okay? I think you're so cute that I want to bite you."

"If a knife or a needle can't even break through," I say, "I hope a bullet can't."

"It'd still hurt if you got shot. The impact of the bullet. Do you bruise?"

"This is still really new to me," I say. "I haven't learned anything about this since it started."

"Look at where you're at now," Somer rubs her foot on me. "It's almost an advantage."

"And I haven't considered the possibility of going back," I say.

"You mean back to Lynn?"

"No, what if my skin changes back?"

Somer turns her attention to the remaining soup in her bowl while her curling toes grip my knee.

"Would you still like me?" I ask. "I'm not even trying to sound insecure."

"I wouldn't leave you if you changed again," Somer says. "I'm not in love with your skin. That'd be a weird thing to fall in love with."

"But you obviously like it."

"Oh, I love it. Sometimes I think about you the way you are and I get a little wet."

"I guess that's how I feel about you too," I say. "But you have more than just nice skin that I like."

"Like what?"

"I mean, if you were in an accident where you ended up losing your ass, thighs, boobs, and your eyes changed color, I wouldn't want to dump you."

"You know, I've never thought to ask what you like about me," Somer says. "I guess it was obvious."

"Mostly you," I say. "I'd still want to live with you if you looked like a Gargoyle. Everyone feels the same in the dark anyway."

"We never do it in the dark."

"I'd say that's a mutually beneficial thing," I say.

"So," Somer points at the TV, "What do you rank the documentary?"

"I'd rather have my eyelids pried open and be forced to watch scat porn."

"Couldn't you have said something milder like *Spice World*?"

"I like *Spice World*," I say. "I used to fantasize about them kidnapping and molesting me."

"Uhh," Somer takes her feet away from me.

"You're kind of like a cross between Baby and Posh Spice."

"We can save the roleplay for when our sex gets stale."

"I've never had stale sex," I say. "Just less sex."

"Hey," Somer says, "Why don't we talk about something more substantial like books or the disadvantages of only cleaning your floor with a Swiffer."

"Should I invest in a mop?" I ask.

"Actually, never mind. You do the cleaning, so you do it how you want to, pumpkin."

"Speaking of being your servant," I say, "What're your professors having you do for the rest of the semester?"

"Well, Dr. Gillis said she don't want to deal with grading us over Zoom, and I haven't practiced in a week. I don't think any of us have, really."

"Pick a piano out and I'll see about getting a cart so we can wheel it into the house," I say.

"I'm not letting you buy me things, Wayne. You paid off my lease. Maybe for Christmas."

"What if I just want a piano for the aesthetic?" I ask.

"It would look better upstairs with the racks of clothes I'm supposed to be buying, thank you."

"Why haven't you ordered anything? You can use my Paypal."

"Because shopping online doesn't work as well when you can't try it before you have to tape the package back together and send it back for a refund."

"I could just pay a store to open so you could shop privately," I say.

"Where am I going to wear any of it?" Somer asks. "We can't go nowhere."

# Chapter 20

"Your Mom is pissed off about that movie they made about you," Dad says. "She stopped watching when they had that girl try to cut you. And she won't talk to Lynn ever again."

Dad doesn't call me often. When we're in person, he usually speaks two sentences within the time span of our visit. I haven't seen Mom in over two weeks, and while I can go without seeing Dad for the predicted eighteen months, I worry I'm losing time with my mother.

"If everyone had done what they oughta done, we wouldn't have this damn virus in the state. You hear about how it spread to Georgia?"

"I don't have my ear to the ground like you, I guess," I say.

"A family came down from New York for a funeral and got everyone there sick. They were hugging and kissing and crying together. Ain't got any sense. If I catch this thing and die, you better cremate my ass. Don't have no funeral."

"You sound unusually spirited," I say.

"Your friend Steve tried getting in touch with me back in January. Flo told him no."

"Steve Sebastian wanted to talk to you?" I ask.

"I don't mean to sound unchristian, but that's a stupid name."

"I suppose it would be unchristian to pick up a journalist and toss him off a bridge."

"Oh, you can't hate a man for doing his job," Dad says. "I don't hate ambulance chasers and bill collectors."

"No?"

"The Lord's gonna have a word or two to say to them on judgement day, Wayne. Steve Sebastian will likely be near the back of the line."

"Alright, Dad," I say. "I think..."

"Wayne," Dad interrupts. "What did I hear about you already having another woman?"

"I don't have any woman because you can't have a woman. There is a woman I love who lives with me. Her name is Somer."

"Were you cheating on Lynn with this woman who's named after a season?"

"It's not spelled like Summer," I say. "I met her before New Years."

"Am I gonna have to put you back in therapy for your bad habit?"

"No, I don't need sex therapy. Bye, Dad."

I didn't go to a therapist for my sex problem so much as lie about going after Dad caught me getting a blow job in my Escort outside our house. Considering I couldn't let my date go down on me and let me toss her salad in the Chick-Fil-A parking lot, I had to make a detour to my childhood home. I thought my parents were asleep, and it seems the feeling of doing something wrong helps me get off. I probably need therapy for recovering from my father seeing me cum in a shocked woman's hair and face. That was an awkward drive back to the Delta-Delta-Delta sorority house.

Dad never thought to ask why I would do such a thing, though. I wouldn't have an answer back then either. Of course, I still lie to people about why I was an English major, and usually in hopes that I'll forget my dreams failed and I had to get a real job.

"So, your dad sounds like he already wants to adopt me as his daughter-in-law," Somer says.

"How much did you hear?" I ask.

"Just what you were saying," Somer says. "Apparently, you need sex therapy."

"Turns out all I needed was to get married," I say. "That'll make or break a sex addict."

"Is that why you're such a freak?"

"Oh, there are people a lot worse than I am," I say.

"I've never had a man use his tongue like a Swiss Army knife, Wayne."

"Have you ever read *Moby Dick*?" I try changing the subject.

"All I'm saying is if you ever break up with me, I'm going to have much higher standards."

"Have you told your parents about me, by the way?"

Somer shuts her laptop and lies down in my lap with the same grin I probably gave Mom when she caught me stealing Big Red gum from Dad's truck. If her parents don't know about me, they're going to be pissed that half the people on the internet knew before them.

"Mama called me last night," She holds my hand. "Daddy went to my apartment yesterday and asked why I wasn't there anymore."

"So?"

"I told them I was living with a man."

"And?"

"They wanted to know who."

"Go on."

"I told them about you, and they coincidently watched the documentary about you, but they had no idea that I was with you when they did."

"How did she take that?" I ask.

"Well, Daddy isn't happy and thinks if you get me pregnant, I'm going to have a mutant baby."

"To be fair," I tilt my head.

"Hey, is your semen green when it comes out at first?" Somer ask.

"Are your parents pissed at you?"

"I had to tell them I was majoring in nursing for three years," Somer says. "I can't tell them anything without them getting pissed."

"Yeah, my parents didn't love that I was an English major."

"Why did you major in English?" Somer asks. "It can't be just because you liked reading."

"I would say that I don't want to talk about it, but that wouldn't be fair. I think most English majors want to be writers."

"You write?" Somer asks.

"No," I say. "Not since about 2012."

"Why'd you stop? I mean, you could be writing now."

"It makes me sound like a kid."

"You're seven years older than me," Somer says. "Don't make me start calling you Daddy."

"See, I did read a lot of books growing up," I say. "But not only novels. When I was a kid-kid, Mom used to sneak me comic books. Dad didn't want me looking at all that, and he wasn't happy when she'd take me to the movies, but he already had plenty to preach at me about. And like any kid who reads comics, I loved Batman."

"I hate to tell you, but a lot of kids like Batman."

"Reading was my escape, but Batman was my real fantasy. More than anything, I wanted to write Batman. When I wasn't reading, I drew my own comics, and I sucked at drawing, so I thought the writing was my strong point. Whenever Mom took me to see a Batman movie, it was like going to church and seeing God. Every day, I heard Dad quote the Bible and talk about people going to Hell, but there's no God in Gotham. Nobody fears God there. Good people don't have to be afraid of Batman either."

"This explains the drawer full of Batman books in the bedroom," Somer says. "I was thinking you were going to ask me to dress up like Catwoman."

"We can table that," I say. "Anyway, I was originally a creative writing minor and took a screenwriting course, and my professor said that I was wasting my time on fan fiction. So, I stopped trying to write Batman and tried to come up with something of my own, and I couldn't, so I changed my minor to film."

"So why don't we watch every Batman movie and the animated series, and you can write a Batman movie for real?"

"How about we watch Tim Burton's *Batman* and you can use my face as a scratching post?"

"Oh, because of pussy," Somer laughs.

My idea for a Batman movie took place after everyone in the rogue's gallery died and Bruce Wayne was older, much like Dark Knight Returns. However, he wasn't super old and merely outlived his former enemies. Instead, he grew so dissatisfied with the justice system never reforming criminals like the Joker that he rounded everyone up in a warehouse one by one, strapped each of them to a post, and delivered a dramatic monologue about how he wasted his life chasing bad guys only to help each of them grow more grotesque. When he started fighting crime in Gotham, there wasn't a Riddler, Penguin, or Harley Quinn. They all existed because of his presence. Once he realized that and saw how they kept getting away with their deeds, Batman decided to burn them all alive. He didn't do it by setting the building on fire, though. Instead, he doused each criminal with gasoline one by one and set them ablaze individually as they all had to witness someone die before he moved onto the next.

Bruce has to bring Batman out of retirement because his old chums start showing up committing petty crimes in Gotham. He thinks he sees the Joker at a bank robbery, but that's not possible. Security cameras catch Riddler stealing insignificant artifacts from a museum. Someone breaks into the zoo and releases the penguins while leaving a dozen open umbrellas hanging in their exhibit. None of these crimes end up with anyone hurt and they're more like old Adam West series schemes.

There's one man behind all of this. He's dressing up to taunt Batman. Earlier in the film, Batman encounters the new police commissioner, Bill Blake, who threatens to have him arrested for nosing into these cases. The twist is that Blake did it all to bait Batman into a trap so he could finally reveal the Dark Knight's real identity.

I can't stress over our parents not liking the idea of this relationship. Parents never think anyone is ever good enough for their child. In the case of my mother and father, I don't believe either of them appreciate me living with another woman so soon after my divorce, and I bet Somer's father is smart enough to know what boys and girls do together when they live together.

Thankfully, the stay at home orders prevent us from meeting each other's parents. As long as they remain healthy, I wouldn't mind spending eighteen months with Somer doing nothing.

"If we get married, are you going to stop fucking me?" Somer asks.

"No," I say. "But you'd have to want to marry me for that to even become a topic of interest."

"Do you see yourself ever getting married again?" Somer asks.

"I always said I wouldn't if Lynn died or something," I say. "I kind of assumed no one would want to marry me unless they had a turtle fetish."

"It's time you found out somehow. I dress up like April O'Neil every Halloween. Would you mind wearing the shell?"

"I'm not getting married in a shell," I say.

"I didn't say I wanted to marry you. I said I wanted you to wear a shell."

"Well, I don't have the mobility for that. Also: Ouch."

"You'll have to propose to me one day and find out, Donatello."

Chapter 21

The only reason business couldn't be done on Skype or something like Zoom years ago is because of this exact scenario. First, Flo can't figure out how to turn on her webcam. Then, she asks if everyone can hear her. There're only two other people on the call besides us. None of the producers are present; just the Fox attorneys assigned to yet another instance of someone threatening to sue them. Because of the virus, we can't meet in person for the foreseeable future, so if this does get in front of a judge, we'll do it online.

"Okay, Mrs. Garner," One of the legal team speaks up, "We see and hear you. Everyone is present for this meeting."

"Alright," Flo says. "Are you ready for me?"

"Yes."

"Upon review of the contract my client, Wayne Pallidus, signed for your production of the *Green* documentary, we stipulated that no other person could accept reimbursement for an appearance in the program. No one informed me or Mr. Pallidus that the former Mrs. Pallidus, Lynn, would appear, so he and the rest of the world got to find out the day the program aired on Hulu. Before moving forward with any legal action, I called this meeting to get clarity regarding why Searchlight violated this agreement."

"Yes, this is Robin Parker, and I am one of the legal representatives of Fox. While we concede to your point that the contract states no other person may accept reimbursement to appear on camera, we have documentation proving that we didn't offer to pay nor did we pay Mrs. Pallidus for her appearance on the program."

"Are you trying to tell me that Lynn appeared without payment?" Flo asks.

"Not from us," Robin says. "The journalist who brought this story to our attention, Mr. Steve Sebastian, paid Mrs. Pallidus from his own pocket to appear on the program. Fox Searchlight productions wants to let Mr. Pallidus know that our company understands his perspective and we're actually going to release a follow up production with his approval with the uncut footage of his interview. No other person will appear to give any other perspective. The reimbursement for an additional production will be discussed later in this meeting or at an arrangement time best fit to Mr. Pallidus's schedule. Furthermore, we have terminated Mr. Benjamin Presswell's employment with our company, and he will no longer be hired for future productions. Since we're transitioning currently due to our new parent company The Walt Disney Company purchasing Fox and Searchlight in 2019, we will no longer employ Mr. Presswell on any production with The Walt Disney Company."

I didn't realize that Ben would get fucked on this, but he must've known about the contract stipulation. From a legal perspective, I suppose it makes sense because his actions were reckless and resulted in this meeting. Steve Sebastian paying Lynn out of his own pocket doesn't surprise me. He likely tried the same with my parents.

"I'm going to chime in here," I say. "We don't need to meet about any follow up or any future production for the uncut footage of the documentary. I don't want anything to do with that."

"Is that going to be a problem, Robin?" Flo asks.

"We were hoping that releasing the uncut footage without any of Mrs. Pallidus's segments would help Mr. Pallidus's story be heard more thoroughly, and the compensation for this release would ease any animosity toward Searchlight."

"Sounds like Searchlight wants to settle before we proceed with any possible legal action," Flo says.

"We did have a discussion about a settlement prior to this meeting and received approval for a specific amount. However, we wanted to offer Mr. Pallidus the opportunity to discuss an additional release with reimbursement akin to his original payment."

I should ask for stock in Disney. Realistically, I don't need more money. My intention wasn't to hoard wealth, though I'm certainly not a billionaire. Before this pandemic began, I saw people like Genevieve and Steve trying profiting off the global damage as if they'd gotten the best stock tip before a market crash. I'm not suffering through any of this. While seeing Lynn hurt me, I'm not going to therapy to cry about it. I live in a nice house, have sex with a beautiful woman, and get to do whatever I want with my life.

"What's the other offer, Robin?" Flo asks.

"We can pull the documentary and offer an additional five million dollars to Mr. Pallidus for our error in judgement."

"Out of curiosity," I say, "Has Hulu netted an increase in subscribers to justify considering the documentary profitable?"

"I don't have that information in front of me," Robin says. "Considering you were paid for your participation and don't have a stake in the documentary's success, I assume you're asking if anyone who has a percentage on the project has received any money?"

"Pretty smart," I say. "More specifically, I was wondering if Steve Sebastian has received any checks."

"Oh, I doubt he's seen a dime from us," Robin says. "He wouldn't receive much even if it was profitable."

"Flo, I'm good with the terms," I say.

"Fax us any necessary documents, Robin," Flo says. "If you wouldn't mind."

"Yes, we'll need a signature from Mr. Pallidus. It can be electronic."

Somer is practicing with her Yamaha keyboard on the coffee table when I come out of my spare room. I step outside to get some air while I get Genevieve on the phone. She may've decided to retire early if her stocks panned out like she hoped. I should probably keep tabs on that myself, but I really don't give a shit.

"Expect another payment from Fox," I say. "Or Disney. Or whoever."

"How much this time?" Genevieve asks.

"Five million, so the same amount after taxes like before. It's kind of ridiculous."

"You're tripping over money now," She says. "Hey, do you think turning green has anything to do with your luck now? Like maybe I should paint myself..."

"No," I say. "But I supposed unrealistic things happen to someone with an unrealistic condition. I don't want to put this in stock. What's going on with property values?"

"Home sales are down, and office space is getting cheap, but I don't think either are good investments right now. Land is always a good investment, though."

"We'll sleep on it until something more exciting happens," I say. "Keep it in my savings for now."

"How's that girlfriend of yours?"

"You saw the doc," I say.

"Let me tell you, Wayne," Genevieve slaps her desk. "Not a soul is on your ex-wife's side when it comes to you moving on."

"I don't think even Lynn is on her side," I say. "Why do you ask?"

"Well, you have money now. I assume she's younger than you. Are you being careful?"

"Are you asking me if I'm having unprotected sex?"

"It's 2020, Wayne. None of my girlfriends carry condoms. We're either on the pill or have an IUD."

"Why are we talking about this?"

"Nothing. I'm just the lady who handles your money."

When I come back inside, Somer is talking to someone on the phone and looking at me as if I brought a cake to a Weight Watchers meeting. She's listening while nodding at the floor. After she tells her *Daddy* that she loves him, I figure he's giving her hell for living with me. I imagine that's something neither of her parents expected.

"How's that going?" I ask.

"Daddy wants to see me," Somer exhales. "He can't be at work right now, so all he has to do is fret over his daughter, I guess."

"Do you think your parents want to meet me?" I ask.

"I suppose introducing you wouldn't dig me any deeper with them."

Somer comes over and puts her hands around the back of my neck.

"I'm almost done with school and I don't ask them for anything, so I shouldn't have to listen to them," She says.

"You're an adult," I nod. "But you love your parents and want their approval. I get that."

"Not really. I love them, but I think Mama regrets having me learn piano. They didn't want me to pursue music because they didn't think there was any money in it. Now I have you and they don't care how much money you have."

"So if it were up to them, you'd be a nurse during a pandemic."

"Right? I'd rather be broke."

"Do you wanna go over there today?" I ask.

"Let me get dressed," Somer says. "You can back out any time. We should make a safe word."

"Do you need a safe word?" I ask. "If I feel like I'm unwanted, I'll just leave."

Despite that Carroll County and Newnan are only thirty minutes away from each other, and Whitesburg's speed trap accounts for an added five minutes, I didn't go to the Coweta area very often growing up. My window into the area was through a local Newnan TV station that Dad sometimes put on when he wanted to take a nap in the living room. SBN wasn't like a Tim and Eric sketch where eccentric people made call-in shows, but there was a guy with a thirty-minute infomercial for his air conditioning business that you wouldn't want to run into in a dark alley.

When I first started hanging out here in college, I noticed something was a little different about the people. While Carroll County definitely has a Walmart crowd, I have never seen someone wearing a Confederate flag hoodie in Target. The same cannot be said about Newnan. There's even a Redneck Gourmet restaurant in downtown Newnan, which isn't a business that would survive in many places, and it's been here for decades. Alan Jackson grew up here and his music was so pervasive in the 90's that even I knew "Chattahoochee," a song that romanticized a river that's thirteen miles from my parents' house and nobody with any sense would actually swim in. Wayne Williams, the Atlanta Child Murderer, dumped bodies in the river too.

What I like about Newnan is that there's a mix of old and new. However, that old is almost like the difference between Alabama and Georgia as soon as you cross state lines. It's that sensibility that allows me to live far enough in the woods for no one on the passing street to see me.

Somer's parents, Perry and Shannon, live in a one story ranch style home on Stonewall Court. I'm not sure if that's one of those generic names used by a developer like Rustic Handle or a reference to Stonewall Jackson. Shannon will likely recognize me from school, but I have no idea what to expect from Perry. I've never heard of someone shooting their daughter's boyfriend around here, but that doesn't mean it won't happen.

The man wearing cargo shorts, Northface vest, and Realtree hat picking at something in the front yard is likely Perry unless the Holly family employs a landscaper who doesn't use a mower. The way he strides over to the Jetta while holding an invisible stick tells me I should've stayed at home.

"That Mexican hater Kemp says we gotta stay six feet apart," Perry says. "Y'all wanna come out back?"

"Okay, Daddy," Somer says.

"I'm Perry, by the way," He waves at me. "Unless there's another green man running around here, I'd say your name is Wayne."

"Nice to meet you," I say. "I actually know your wife, Shannon..."

"Yeah, she about broke a window when you came on the TV. *That's Wayne! I know him! I know him!*"

On the patio, there's a metal table and matching chairs with plenty of distance on each end. Considering Perry used an oddly accurate yet politically incorrect way to describe the governor, I assume he's not against the COVID-19 regulations like wearing a mask or not invading strangers' personal space.

"Hey Shannon," Perry calls inside, "Your college sweetheart just showed up. Oh, Somer's here too."

"Y'all want something to drink?" Her voice calls back.

"We'll take a Diet Coke, Mama," Somer shouts.

"You know anything about yodeling?" Perry gestures. "Farmers used to sing to each other because of the distance between their land. What you just witnessed was like a primitive form of rednecks hollering at one another."

"My dad is a minister," I say, "So I heard plenty of hollering growing up."

Shannon appears with two cans of Diet Coke, which she sets down in the middle of the table. I reach over to grab them while realizing neither Shannon nor Perry are smiling. Shannon also avoided looking at me when she came outside.

"How long you been seein' him?" Perry asks.

"Almost four months," Somer says.

"Four months and now you're living together?" Shannon asks.

"My roommates left, and I was the only remaining tenant, so Wayne offered to pay the rest of my lease and let me move in with him."

"So you quit your job," Shannon says, "Did you also drop out of school?"

"I am graduating this semester. Why would I do that?"

"You might as well be signing up to strip on Mars," Perry says. "You're living with a man who looks like an alien from *Futurama*."

"First of all, I'm an adult, and neither of you support me financially," Somer says. "You don't get a say in what I do with my life. Second of all, insulting Wayne doesn't make you very endearing to me. He hasn't done anything wrong."

"What happens if you get pregnant with him?" Shannon asks.

My phone starts vibrating, so I hold it up for everyone to see before I dart back to the front yard. On the third vibration, I see that it's Lynn calling me. The last time we spoke, she came to my house with divorce papers and said she didn't want to see me ever again as if I'd found her illegitimate sister and posted us humping on Facebook. Of course, she hasn't really left my life thanks to the documentary.

"Yeah?" I answer.

"Wayne," Lynn says. "Is this a bad time?"

"What can I do for you, Lynn?"

"No one told me you didn't want me to be in the documentary, so I apologize for that. I needed the money and that Steve guy talked me into it."

"Yeah, I heard he paid you himself," I say.

"What he said was that he was going to pay me first and I'd get paid again by the studio later."

"Well, sounds like you got duped," I say. "How much did he give you?"

"Two grand. You know me. That lasted me all of five minutes."

"I'm sure retail therapy helped you some."

"I was feeling better until I couldn't leave the apartment. Now I'm stuck here unless I can find a new place before the eviction ban lifts."

"If you need help, I can find you a place."

"No, Wayne. I don't want anything from you. I severed that tie when we got divorced."

"I suppose I should be more upset about that," I say.

"Having seen the documentary, I'd say you found a way to fix that pretty quickly. Is she younger than me, Wayne?"

I'm not responding to that. Lynn can lay a trap, but I can hang up and block her number. Steve Sebastian did her wrong, yet I don't know why she'd take his money and not accept some from me. I wanted to help her before the divorce too.

"He asked me where you live," Lynn says. "I told him if he was such a good journalist, why couldn't he figure that out?"

"Hmm."

"He had pictures of you with your new girlfriend. She's pretty."

"Why ask if she's younger than you, then? Wasn't that obvious? Did he sit there showing you his whole Camera Roll?" I ask. "Does he have pictures of my asshole too?"

"I've seen enough of your asshole, so I would just slide past those."

"Well, it was fun catching up, Lynn," I say. "Do you feel vindicated now?"

"No."

"I'm sorry things haven't gotten that much better for you. If you need my help, you can call anytime."

Perry is watching me from the side of the house. When I pocket my phone, he's glaring with a heavy exhale. Unless Somer told them about our sex life, I assume he'd looking for a reason to hate me and that phone call gave him some kind of suspicion. Me saying anything about it would only confirm that paranoia.

"Who you talking to?" He asks.

"How long were you listening?" I ask.

"Sounded like you were talking to a woman."

"Yeah, I've met a few of those in my life," I say. "My mom is a woman, believe it or not. So is my dental hygienist."

"You weren't talking to your mama, boy."

"Turns out, Somer isn't the only woman I know."

He strides to me, and the only way I can avoid this is if I jump out of the way and run. Then he'd probably chase me, and that's not a good look. When he hits me, and he gets me in the left eye as soon as I complete that thought, Somer will only resent him. It's not my intention to create a rift in their family, but she is an adult and isn't ruining her life with me. I'm surprised they didn't bring up the seven year age gap. The internet probably did when someone posted pictures of us together. According to Twitter, every man who dates a younger woman is a cradle-robbing-pervert who deserves to be hanged. Meanwhile, they'd all let Leonardo DiCaprio and Pedro Pascal use them like a ragdoll.

"Daddy," Somer emerges.

"Perry," Shannon follows. "Why'd the hell you hit that boy?"

"I'd never hit a boy," Perry says. "That's a man, and he's fucking my daughter."

"Oh, thank you for acknowledging my manhood," I say from the ground.

He kicks me back over and lands another punch in my jaw. Defending myself wouldn't bode well, especially on someone else's property. He's got at least fifty pounds on me anyway.

"He's got enough money for ten lawyers, Perry," Shannon says, "And you just assaulted him on our front lawn."

"I might just let him sue you too, Daddy," Somer says.

"Hold on," I say.

They stop after I hit pause on my social remote by being the helpless green man with dirt the back of his shirt. Perry wants to knock me back on the ground, but he's already gotten two hits in, and a third would make him look like a bully.

"I appreciate you welcoming me onto your property," I say. "Despite that I'll probably have a bruised face for a while, I am not going to sue anyone. I happen to want you to like me, even if you merely tolerate me for the sake of your daughter."

"Perry," Shannon grabs his arm, "Apologize."

"He was talking to another woman on the phone," Perry says.

"Yes," I say. "My ex-wife called to say she was sorry about the documentary. She wasn't supposed to be in it and she got tricked into doing it. She knows about Somer and has no interest in seeing me again. In fact, she finds me disgusting. From what you said about me earlier, I'm surprised you'd hit me since my alien disease might rub off on you."

"Nah, I figured I was safe since Somer hasn't turned technicolor yet," Perry says.

"I told you to say sorry, Perry."

"Goddamn it," He says. "Alright. I'm sorry for hitting you."

"You know what," I say, "I don't need an apology. Your daughter deserves one, though. She is the kindest person in the world, which tells me she had two very good parents. Unless you're evil clones of Perry and Shannon Holly, I know you must be kind too."

"Hell, Wayne," Shannon says, "You already knew I was a pistol."

We're all smiling, and Somer walks over to me as if taking a side. She pulls my hand out of my pocket to hold to make a deliberate statement.

"I'm not just fucking your daughter," I say. "I'm trying to take care of her."

"And we actually appreciate that," Shannon says. "We know you got money and she's doing fine, but we're confused. She didn't tell us she was moving, we don't know where she lives, and..."

"Come over then," I say.

Someone looks at us from the window, and I'm assuming the little eyes belong to Stevie, Somer's little brother. His phone appears when he presses it against the window to take a picture.

"You can follow us right now," I say, "Or we can have a cook out."

"That's sweet of you," Shannon says. "Maybe once the virus isn't so bad."

"I didn't even leave a mark on him," Perry gestures.

Somer pulls me to her by my chin and nods.

"Still the same shade of green," Somer says.

"I was wondering what would happen after I saw you not get cut on that movie," Perry says.

## Chapter 22

"There's something about having a daddy in the service," Somer says. "How do you imagine my life was like before I went to school?"

"I'm guessing it wasn't typical?" I ask. "Or normal?"

"What's typical or normal even mean?" She asks. "I told you we lived on a base until I was almost eight. What are our formative years, Wayne? Is it when we're real little and learning to talk and walk without falling on our face? If you cut us away from the life we know early on, does it hurt less than when it happens later?"

"So much of what damages us can be from our own fingertips," I say. "What happened after your parents moved off the base?"

Somer turns onto the road that leads to my private neighborhood. She was quiet when we left her parents' house, and she might wonder if I hold her father's actions against her. I bet Perry held onto that punch for years. Having a pretty daughter with the eyes of many boys and men on her while losing her to adulthood probably hurts. That gesture wasn't aimed at me directly, though it felt like it at the time.

"I couldn't keep a friend for long on the base," Somer says. "I guess I'm used to people coming in and out of my life. Mostly, I'm used to the going."

"What was your rock growing up?" I ask.

"Music. Mama let me have my own CD player, and I'd listen to her albums in my room. Well, you know, they were my grandmother's first. She had *Songs From the Big Chair* and all the Zeppelin albums. Van

Halen, Eagles, Skynyrd, and Clapton too. I didn't like them as much, though."

"What is it about that album?"

I have to get out of the car with my cap on and head down to put the code into the gate since we forgot to bring the remote. I need to get one made for Somer. No one drives by in the time it takes me to hop back in the Jetta.

"How come you didn't listen to music growing up?" Somer asks.

"If my parents didn't play it, I didn't hear it unless it was in a movie," I shrug. "I guess I could've sought it out if it really mattered to me."

"There's a difference between when a song plays on the radio than hearing it on a full album, you know? An album is like a story. A book with music. The best ones take you on a journey. I guess I just liked how things started and ended on *Songs From the Big Chair*."

"You ever think about how it starts with a song called 'Shout,' and ends with 'Listen'?"

"Well, Wayne Pallidus. You did pay attention."

"I guess I kinda liked it."

"You tell me, Mr. English major. Why does it start and end the way it does?"

"You probably know more about it than I do."

"That first song is about primal scream therapy. Most of the words on the last song are random African things like 'chicken.' Sounds good, but I think the most important part is how 'Broken' plays again after 'Head Over Heels.' Obsession doesn't lead to anything productive when it's unrequited."

"Sounds like you loved someone before you met me," I tease.

I reach on top of the fridge for the Bisquick before taking the chicken and eggs out. Tossing some bread crumbs in the bowl with the white powder, I add salt, pepper, garlic powder, and onion powder before coating the tenders and testing the vegetable oil. As a side, I have to time the Velveeta shells just right because I hate lukewarm food.

"Who was your first love?" Somer asks.

"Lynn," I say. "Do you want honey mustard or ranch for your chicken?"

"Whatever you're having is fine. Lynn was your first?"

"I didn't really realize that until I lost her. I knew I was in love with her, but there's a difference between what I felt for her and everyone before. All the other girls... Look, I don't want to sound a certain way. I guess sexist?"

"What do you want to say?" Somer asks.

"I used to be like Johnny Appleseed and didn't have an orchard I wanted to settle down on until I met Lynn."

"What made her special?"

Lynn was more than attractive. She kept up with me. But sometimes two souls hook on one another. What made Lynn special? I kept coming back to her in my mind in a way I didn't with the others.

"I was almost out of school," I say. "My parents were concerned about my running around."

"That why your dad mentioned sex therapy?"

"I didn't go to therapy, but I was aware I may have been burning a rope I shouldn't have been climbing in the first place. So, I needed a person. A friend I could keep. Lynn was the first woman I went out with that was my best friend."

Somer's eyes change the subject when she sees the food. I can make baked macaroni and cheese that would make your grandmama's cooter swell in her coffin, but Velveeta did something right. Maybe it's the child in us. Throw the right combination of chemicals and cheese together, and something magnificent happens.

"You should let me make dinner tomorrow," Somer says. "I haven't cooked for you since our second date."

"What do you wanna make?" I ask.

"Oh, before we decide on dinner," Somer sets her fork down, "I'm really sorry about Daddy."

"Didn't leave a mark," I wink.

"Yeah, but that hurt me too. He's never hit one of my boyfriends before. He hasn't met most of them, though."

"I'm sure my dad will punch you in the face too," I say.

"I bet my daddy could beat up your daddy."

Once the food's gone and we return to a state of catatonic fullness, I take it upon myself to pull on Somer's ankle so she slides onto her back after sitting on the couch. Crawling in the space between her and the cushions, I lie on my side while resting my face on her chest.

"Who was your first love?" I ask.

"You."

"There must be someone you thought you loved."

"Sure," Somer says. "I guess it wasn't that long ago. I was still in high school, and there was this guy, Brandon, who worked at Barnes and Noble. He wasn't even in school. He just worked there."

"How old was he?" I ask.

"He was nineteen and I'd just turned seventeen."

"So you have a type."

"I thought he was smart because he liked to read and worked in the bookstore. He was my first."

"Your first?"

"I told you it's a bad idea to sleep around here. I wouldn't do it with someone I didn't know loved me."

"So what happened?"

"He got his GED and applied to UGA. I figured we could keep going because Athens isn't that far."

"You should've gone to Athens before you figured on that," I say. "There's nothing to do there. He cheat on you?"

"Probably. Does it count as cheating if he ghosts me?"

"Damn," I say.

There's an alert that someone is at the gate. I pull up my security app and see Steve Sebastian looking at the camera while trying to use the keypad. One cool feature is that I can sound an alarm that sounds like a banshee having a panic attack. He jumps back, and Somer looks at me as if we're under attack.

"Stay here," I say. "Our friend Steve has found our location."

"Don't go talk to him here," Somer says.

"Oh, I'm not going to do much talking at all."

Turning the alarm off, I turn on the intercom as I'm opening the case for my rifle next to the front door.

"May I help you?" I ask.

"Wayne," Steve throws up his arms as if he won the lottery. "Turns out I'm not such a bad journalist after all, huh?"

"The gate opens toward the house," I say. "Would you mind standing toward the center?"

"So you are going to come talk to me, huh?"

Aiming the barrel near the tree line, I let out a round, which echoes loud enough for people in 2010 to hear it. Through my phone and in the distance, I hear Steve curse and slam his car door.

"If you come back," I say, "I hope you've made arrangements with your family ahead of time."

"What are you doing?" Somer comes outside.

"I'm done now," I smile.

"Use some of that aggression on me instead. You're gonna make some old lady poop her Depends."

## Chapter 23

I felt like someone who witnessed a murder from a distance and couldn't call for help in time. It was over a year ago in March. I was at work and every few moments, I remembered I was going to be a father. Every day, my colleagues told me, "When you're a daddy..." and my parents were looking forward to babysitting when Lynn and I needed time. A baby makes so many people happy merely by existing. They're celebrities that everyone passes by with a smile or stops to talk to you about them.

Sometimes, providers bill out a 99215 for a claim, and the insurance company denies the code because they don't want to pay the contracted amount. In terms of E&M codes, 99205 and 99215 are the highest amount a doctor can bill. The numbers at the end essentially signify the amount of time the provider spends evaluating the patient. Now, we've all been to the doctor and know we spend most of our time in the waiting room or sitting in an empty exam room waiting for the guy or lady in a white jacket to speak to us for three minutes before leaving. The E&M codes ending in 5 mean the provider saw the patient for an hour or more.

Claims analysts with less experience will make the mistake of calling about a 99215 denial and spend an hour on the phone while someone from India reads from a script regarding the expectations for reimbursing such a code. They'll say they need medical records to justify the "high complexity and research" involved. Aetna of California were sued for not reviewing medical records. Most fax machines at big companies feed right into a trash can. I've even sent faxes to "active" numbers with disconnected machines.

I was printing the entire patient history for BCBS to justify this 99215 to send in an expandable white envelope with a certified mail slip. The mail lady got irritated, but the best way to have BCBS pay any denied claim was to send every record you had on file. I had BCBS reps from all over the country tell me this. It's as if the people who reviewed the appeals just threw up their hands when they saw the pile of documents.

While standing at the printer, Lynn sent me a text to call her. Now, I like to keep my home and work life separate. I spoke to Lynn on breaks sometimes, but she had a bad habit of wanting to spend a lot more than fifteen minutes with me. Other times, we'd get into an argument over something stupid and I'd go back to my desk pissed off.

Stepping into the break room, I asked Siri to call Lynn while worrying someone would mess with my print job.

"Wayne," Lynn answered, "I'm driving to the ER. Can you leave early?"

"Why are you going to the ER?"

"I'm bleeding. I went to the bathroom and it started coming out like I was having a heavy period."

"Do you think you might just be having your period while pregnant?"

"Are you coming?"

I sent an email to Lisa before clocking out and passing the smokers as they came into the office. The hospital was less than ten minutes away, but the local high school was letting classes out, so I had to drive around and ended up arriving in the parking garage fifteen minutes later.

By the time I walked into the hospital, Lynn texted me that she was still in the waiting room, but a nurse called us in just as I got to sit down. Before we were in the patient room, the nurse confirmed it was likely a miscarriage based on the symptoms.

After a week of awkwardly telling people she'd lost the baby, my colleagues, our friends, and family went back to status quo. Meanwhile, Lynn wasn't sleeping and put in her notice at work.

I'm not one of those people who actually believes getting pregnant is a tragedy when you're young, unless the mother is barely in her teens. People act like anyone who is sixteen through nineteen having a child is the worst possible thing that could happen. It's not ideal, and I certainly believe there should be done more to educate kids so they don't get pregnant before they're adults and ready to support a child. But it's still not a bad thing. Birth and death are unavoidable, have their positive aspects, and I found myself envying the stories about having sex one night in a backseat and a childbirth happening nine months later.

But I buried that experience like the people around me. Lynn couldn't. It's not that losing our child caused her depression alone. She was looking forward to being a mother, but there wasn't anything else in her life bringing her joy.

I'm considering how she shut me out of her life when I hear Somer in the bathroom this morning. It's unlikely that she has food poisoning. No, it wouldn't be a bad thing if she was expecting, but my memory of not only losing an unborn child but also my wife and best friend leads me to fear the potential failure of another relationship.

"Are you breathing okay?" I knock on the door.

"Yeah, I'll be fine," Somer says.

"I can Doordash us a pregnancy test from Walgreens," I say.

Opening the bathroom door, Somer is swishing Listerine in her mouth and looking at me as if I'm dumb to assume her second day of throwing up in the morning isn't somehow linked to pregnancy.

"I'll go get one," Somer says. "Do you want anything from the store?"

"If you're pregnant, you shouldn't risk getting sick," I say.

"Okay, dear," Somer grabs my wrists, "We don't know that I'm pregnant until I take a test or go to the doctor."

"Do you have health insurance?" I ask.

"I'm on my father's plan," Somer nods.

"Who is his policy carrier?" I ask.

"Humana, I think."

"Is it an HMO?"

"Yeah, it kinda sucks," Somer shrugs.

"Well, obviously I'm going to pay for everything."

"What?"

"Like the doctor visits and hospital."

"Wayne, we don't know that I'm pregnant yet."

An hour later, I'm drinking the Pibb Zero and licking the dust off a Dorito while Somer pees in a cup. I figured after our first time, she was on birth control and I didn't need to use the condoms I kept in the drawer. Her having a period didn't even faze me as an indication that she wasn't on anything.

She steps out of the bathroom and looks at me from down the hall. Stomping toward me, Somer holds up the two tests she took, and they both read Pregnant.

"Fuck," I say. "I don't know how to react because we've never talked about this. Do you want this? Is this okay?"

"Well, let's talk," Somer sits next to me at the bar.

"You aren't on birth control, are you?" I ask.

"I used to get the shot," Somer says. "I stopped in November."

"Did you think it would keep working?"

"No."

"So, do you want to have a kid with me?"

"Do you want to have a kid with me?" Somer asks.

"I asked first."

"But we both know there's a right and wrong answer. The wrong answer is when we don't have the same answer."

"Okay, I didn't plan on this happening, obviously," I say. "But, I kinda knew what I was in for when I didn't pull out."

"Same," Somer nods.

"Which part?"

"Both?"

"So, we're doing this," I say.

Four months ago, I was newly divorced and decided to go into a grocery store because I liked the name and wanted to see how people reacted to me. Had Somer not offered me a cart for a bunch of crap I bought for an air fryer I got for Christmas, this child wouldn't exist. Despite that I don't like the Bible and organized religion, I still have faith and believe in purpose. I was meant to exist. My conception wasn't a mistake. That means I grew up, got married, evolved into a green man, and lost my previous life to begin a new one with Somer.

Admittedly, I have other questions and concerns. Despite that we're adults, we can defy our parents all we wish but we can't stop them from disowning us. If I don't marry Somer and she gives birth to our child, then I'm dead to Dad and he won't allow Mom to speak to me.

Getting married so quickly will cast Somer in a bad light for the outside world. With people like Steve Sebastian always creeping around, there's no way people won't find out I married the woman I mentioned in the documentary. Somer might go shopping one day or fill her car up only for someone to hurl insults at her. That affects her mental health, and I am all too aware that I need to prioritize my partner's wellbeing for both of our sakes.

Furthermore, my celebrity status puts my child at risk. Of course, people are wondering if our baby will be green. I'm not even sure how Somer feels about that.

"What are you thinking?" Somer asks.

"That we have more to talk about," I say.

"You don't seem happy, but I'm sure I don't either."

"You might be mirroring me, though. I'm sorry. I want to be a father, and if I had to pick anyone in the world to raise a child with, it'd be you."

Somer kisses me, and the sweetness of her innocence from only a few months ago is replaced with an element of fury. We're still in the phase of the relationship where we're fucking all the time and getting along. A child is going to change that. She's awoken that part of me I suppressed with Lynn. Yesterday when I came with her, there was a mild pain. I'm doing stretches and Kegels to help with that aspect, but I'm not about to stop trying to break something just because there's something growing inside her.

"I love you," I say. "I know what your intentions have been, but I need something right now."

"Yeah?"

"There's something we haven't talked about at all," I say. "I'm not about to ask you. I don't want to ask you. I want you to compel me. Make me."

"Make you?"

Grabbing Somer by the arm, I walk her to the couch and pull her weight on top of me. Her lips press so firmly that my teeth dig into the front of my mouth. Of course, if Somer wants me to do the traditional proposal, I'll get her the ring, we'll hire a chef, have dinner outside, and I'll go down on one knee. However, nothing about our relationship is akin to normalcy.

Taking off her shirt, Somer pulls herself off me so I can take off my pants and boxers while her breasts fall out of her bra, and the sight of them make me want to abandon this to press her back against the arm rest and fuck them until I finish on her chest and neck. Instead, I put my hands under my back and let her start rubbing.

"Oh, you're trying to get out of popping the question," She says. "You're right, we do have more to talk about."

Squeezing my swollen head with her thumb and forefinger, blood pushes down my shaft as Somer licks the base with the tip of her tongue.

"If I'm going to have your baby, you have to give me everything I ask for."

"When have I told you no?" I ask.

"I can't give you the chance to ever say no."

With her lips kissing up, Somer sucks the side of my head as if preventing the edge of a popsicle from dribbling on her hand. Despite that I asked for this knowing the outcome, I really want her to put me in her mouth.

"You can't get out of marrying me," Somer says. "You have to."

If I give in too soon, the anticipation won't build enough. I'm not doing this for a blowjob. I'm making sure that even when we're exchanging vows, there's the little secret that I didn't have a choice. Somer wanted me and made it happen. Part of me wants her to own me. She can use my dick as her property and see me as an object she can fuck whenever. This notion slightly conflicts with her wanting me to dominate her most of the time and the pleasure I get from her begging me to cum inside her. The point is I want this to be part of our story and therefore keep our relationship feeling like we're always doing something we shouldn't rather than a sweet romantic story that eventually fizzles.

"You think I'm going to let you cum at all without giving me an answer?" Somer presses my dick against my stomach.

"Don't," I say.

"Then you know you can't get out of this."

"Alright."

"No, what do I want to hear?"

"I'll marry you," I say.

"Uh uh," She says. "It's not about you telling me you'll marry me. You want to marry me."

"Yes."

"Say it."

"I do," I say. "I want to marry you."

Somer lets go of me and climbs on with her thighs holding me in place as she rubs her panties against my shaft.

"If you're going to cum, it's going to be in me."

# Chapter 24

"You can't have a wedding now," Dad says. "You can't even get married in a courthouse with this Corona business still going on."

"Well, I happen to know a minister," I say, "And he can sign the certificate that I take to the courthouse."

"Good luck with that."

"Dad, you're the only minister I know."

"I'm not doing a wedding where everyone is gonna end up sick or dying."

"I never said there was going to be a wedding. We need to get married, though."

"What for? You haven't even known this girl for six months. You're just gonna end up in the same position you were in December. She's going to get tired of you, outgrow you, and wanna take half your money. I mean, ain't you thought about this?"

Luckily, I knew better than to call Dad about this with Somer present. I'm in the Volvo, and had to turn the AC on since Georgia Aprils can be a hot bitch. While Somer claims she doesn't need an actual wedding, we don't have a choice when the world is falling apart and we have a deadline. Namely, we need to get married this month so when we eventually tell our families about the baby, they won't assume we're only getting hitched for the sake of preventing social shame.

"And I'm not stupid," Dad says. "You probably got her pregnant, didn't you?"

"What?" I tap the steering wheel to sell my surprise.

"I saw a picture of her on the internet, boy. She looks more fertile than Eden before those two mouth breathing Neanderthals ate an apple and landed us all in this rundown motel room when we could've been in the penthouse."

"Is this something you've said during a sermon?" I ask. "Your metaphors need work."

"I'm not letting your mother go out and get sick just cause her son don't know it's a sin to shack up with a woman seven years younger than him and get her pregnant."

"Dad," I say, "She's not pregnant."

"I'm marking the calendar," Dad says. "If she has a baby in December or before, I know you're a lie."

"Why can't you just do this for me?" I ask. "It just has to be you, Mom, Percy, Shannon, and Stevie. I have plenty of space on my property for no one to have to touch one another."

"When is this sin fest supposed to take place?" Dad asks. "I have to fit you in between telling your mother her son probably knocked up a girl we've never met and facing my congregation after having performed such a ceremony."

"You forgot the infant sacrifice to Satan," I say. "That's on April twenty-ninth."

"Wayne, there are other ministers out there who can do this for you."

I hoped that Dad would agree to do this without hesitation, especially if he suspects I got Somer pregnant. He was supportive of my transformation, but he turned it into a religious thing. I thought if I'd told him about Somer's pregnancy or having a child out of wedlock, he'd disown me. Instead, he's trying to avoid me entirely. Mom hasn't spoken to me on the phone since early March, so he's been my only way in.

"Dad, if I'd ever gone to therapy for any issues in my life," I say, "You'd be the number one topic. I don't ask you for anything. I never have. I've always gone to Mom for help. As my father, you should've agreed to this before I even finished my question."

"Well, if you have such a problem with me, stop calling."

He hangs up before I do. There's no way I can postpone the baby, so I can't really delay getting married. Somer and I both want it to happen even though we know it's soon. Before I make it back into the house to talk to her, my phone starts shaking in my pants. Flo is calling.

"Yes ma'am?" I answer.

"Wayne, we're gonna need to get you an agent, because now Viacom is sending me inquiries about you."

"Right to business," I say. "What does Viacom want?"

"They want to film a reality show pilot for you. I told them you might not be interested."

"I'm not," I say.

But even though I have money, I still have a baby on the way and no new source of income other than the potential I have to sell stock. When I set everything up with Genevieve, I did so with the understanding that it was for me. We didn't factor in a new wife and child. Still, Viacom wanting me to be on MTV or whatever feels like exploitation.

"Do you want to hear the terms?" Flo asks.

"Okay," I say.

"They'll fly you to Los Angeles, provide you a place to live during filming, and it's only for a week of shooting."

"For one episode?"

"Do you maybe wanna think it over?"

"Let me ask you, Flo," I say. "You're smarter than me. What do you think I should do? I have a whole situation going on at home. I just got off the phone with my dad, and he doesn't want to speak to me anymore. I have to get married in the next month because, and this stays between you and me, my girlfriend is expecting."

"Oh, congratulations," Flo says. "Well if you have a baby on the way, you can never have too much money."

"How much are they offering for a pilot?"

"A hundred thousand for one episode. The rep told me if you have someone living with you, they'd throw in twenty five for their appearance."

"Alright, let me talk to Somer," I say.

"A baby!" Flo says. "I don't know what is wrong with your daddy, but he'll come around. Especially if your mama finds out about that baby."

Somer is on a Zoom call with one of her professors when I come inside, so I grab a Coke Zero and sit on the other side of the couch off camera. For once, I can use my mother's line of giving good news and bad news.

"What'd he say?" Somer asks.

"I had two phone calls," I say. "After I got off the phone with Dad, Flo called me about something. So, Dad is pissed at me, and I told him I only expect so much from him, so he told me to not call him anymore. When I spoke to Flo, she said he'd probably get over it eventually."

"Eventually?" Somer asks. "Babe, I really want your parents to like me. Do you think he'd feel better if he punched me in the face?"

"He'd probably just call you a harlot or whore," I say. "He's a real gentleman that way."

"What'd Flo call about?"

"Oh, Viacom wants to do a reality show pilot with me, and I told her I wasn't interested, but that I'd talk to you."

"I agree. We're too boring for a reality show," Somer says. "I bet the pay is shit too."

"Here's my thinking: They're paying for our trip and providing us with a house for a week. I get a hundred thousand and you get twenty five, so we're basically getting paid to take a vacation."

"I don't want to fly," Somer says. "The virus."

"What if we drove?"

"We couldn't get there in time."

"What if we left early and took a road trip. See the country while everyone is still paranoid about leaving the house."

"I mean, I like that idea," Somer holds up her hands. "But what about getting married?"

"Maybe your dad could beat up my dad and then he'd have to marry us?" I ask.

"I think the time for dad jokes is done, sugar pudding," Somer says. "Can we get married if your parents don't want to come?"

My spouse is supposed to come before everyone. My relationship with Dad has always been broken, so I didn't expect the hinges to fall off. If God asked him to sacrifice me as a test, Dad would stain his kitchen floor with my blood before God could tell him Sike. So much of his traditionalism is convenient for him and puts Mom at a disadvantage.

"If Dad misses this, he only has himself to blame," I say. "Do you want to do Los Angeles?"

Somer shakes her head. I don't want to be on camera again either. The idea wasn't even quaint for a moment.

"Here's my idea," Somer says. "We do a road trip for our honeymoon. If people actually want a reality show from you, we should join TikTok. And if you want to make extra money, which we don't need, you can do Cameos."

"I don't think kids want to watch me," I say.

"Umm, kids love you," Somer says. "They think you look like you're from Roblox."

"That's not a real thing."

"It is, and there're a lot of adults on TikTok now."

Somer opens her app, types in something, and turns her phone around to show me a woman in a bikini dancing to a Doja Cat song.

"And if you go to her profile, she has a link to her OnlyFans," Somer says. "Wanna subscribe?"

"How do we do this?"

We go upstairs to Somer's room and she sits me at the piano before handing me some of her Raybans. This seems cheesy and childish to me, and I wouldn't post anything to TikTok if my nuts depended on such a foolish gesture. However, I probably trust my twenty-one year old fiancé without an engagement ring too much, but the worst that can happen is I'm a little embarrassed. The documentary with Lynn's surprise segments did me dirty enough.

Conceptually, me playing a piano very badly is only mildly funny if you're nine. Somer says she can dub in some pretty music after. Turning to the camera, I take off the shades as if what happened was really awesome and not an out-of-touch twenty-eight year old's attempt at being cool.

"Hello," I say, "My name is Wayne, and you probably know me as the Hulu mascot."

Somer bites her lip to keep from laughing. I assume that's a bad thing and this is just as cringy as I thought.

"This will either blow up or no one will see it," Somer says.

## Chapter 25

Given that people are discovering Fleetwood Mac through TikTok, including myself, Somer suggested we speak to a Wiccan priestess because being witchy is in. Plus, getting married by a witch might piss off Dad enough to either step in or regret driving us to taking such a drastic measure. More than likely, he'll cut me out of his will and donate all of his estate to the church.

We trek to Franklin, which is only distinguishable for having police pulling cars over to make money for the town, and having a Piggly Wiggly. Allegedly, there's a Mexican restaurant somewhere. The GPS takes us to a red brick house on a residential street rather than a dirt road leading to a rusted trailer home or tent. Somer plays "Gold Dust Woman" as we pull up.

Margaret Anne greets us with a green mask on, which feels a little on the nose for both of us. Somer bought us special masks from Amazon with filters on each side to keep our breath from running back into our eyes.

"Wayne and Somer, I presume?" Margaret asks.

"Yes, ma'am," I say.

"I just put on a kettle," She motions for us to follow her inside.

Sitting at a table that Vikings probably carried over on a rowboat, Somer and I accept green tea with honey as Margaret sets a manual down and flips to a random page.

"I once married a couple standing on Mayhayley Lancaster's grave," She says. "I had to burn sage throughout this house for a month afterward."

"Sounds smelly," Somer says.

"How long you two been engaged?"

Somer holds up her hand, which is bare.

"You're supposed to buy the ring before asking a woman to marry you," Margaret says.

"She convinced me through other means," I say. "Most of the local jewelers are closed."

"Have you never heard of the internet? Anyway, when is the wedding date?"

"Whenever," I say. "Whatever works for you within the week."

"Wayne, I don't perform ceremonies for men held at gunpoint."

"We will buy a ring today," Somer says. "And we'll get married ASAP."

"I also perform funeral rites if that's of interest to you."

"We're planning a road trip for this weekend or next weekend," I say. "It's supposed to be like our honeymoon."

"She must suck a mean dick," Margaret says. "Or you have a big green dick."

"Wow," I say.

"He's also good at sucking things," Somer says. "We're really getting married because of his feet. They really do it for me."

"Who is attending this ceremony, by the way?"

"My parents," Somer says.

"Is Wayne an orphan?"

"My father is a minister," I say. "He can no longer condone my sinful life of muff diving."

"You say that, but the hardcore Christians are the real freaks-in-the-sheets," Margaret says. "Where is the ceremony being held?"

"My parents' backyard," Somer says.

"I'm sorry," Margaret gestures, "Do you two not have any friends?"

The one jewelry store open in Carroll County is Pendleton on the square. When we walk inside, the man sitting in the back stands up and looks at me harder than if I'd come in with an AK47. He doesn't even greet us. Somer walks to the rings as I enter a staring competition with a guy with a skullet and mustache.

"We're here for rings," I say. "I imagine you sell a few of those?"

"Is your name Wayne?" He asks.

"Yes," I say. "You've heard of me?"

"I saw you on TikTok this morning," He puts on a mask. "My daughter showed me."

"What's your name?"

"Clarence."

"Are you able to resize rings quickly, Clarence?"

"We have nothing else to do, so yes. Were you looking for just the lady, or also yourself?"

"If you have any wedding bands for men, sure."

Somer could pick the biggest diamond they sell, but a store like this isn't going to carry a rock the size of a dime. Instead, she likes a traditional looking set while selecting a white gold band for me. As Clarence seems surprised that my card goes through for three grand, he writes down Somer's ring size.

"I can have them ready today if you're still going to be in town."

"Sure, we can kill time," I say.

"Do you have a dress?"

"I've never worn a dress," I say.

"I mean for her."

"No," Somer says. "And he doesn't have a tux either."

"You know there's a bridal shop down the block," Clarence says. "The Squire Shop is closed, but the ladies who run the bridal shop couldn't afford to stay shut down."

"You should drop me off there," Somer says. "Go see about your Dad."

"Don't tell me your father doesn't know," Clarence asks.

"Oh, he does. He wishes he didn't know."

I wouldn't go see my parents if Somer hadn't suggested the idea. I doubt she can pick out a dress and get fitted in the time it takes Dad to slam the door in my face. Pulling up to their rear driveway reminds me of driving home from school in the afternoons and going straight to my room.

Before I can get to the backdoor, Mom looks out the window and unlocks the deadbolt before sliding outside as if we have an arranged secret meeting. Her hair is longer than usual and she's wearing her glasses instead of contacts, and she's wearing purple sweatpants.

"Oh dang it, I don't have a mask handy," She says.

"We'll stand six feet away from each other," I say. "You doing okay?"

"Yeah," She looks me up and down. "You?"

"I'm getting married this week," I say.

"This week? What day?"

"Apparently it depends on when Somer gets her dress," I say. "It was going to be tomorrow, but we're just getting married in her backyard."

"How far along is she?"

"Why do you and Dad assume she's pregnant?"

Mom crosses her arms like a breeze came through and gives me the same look as when I'd come home late.

"So, I guess I'm stupid," She says.

"I asked Dad to perform the ceremony," I say. "He told me not to talk to him again."

"Who is going to marry you then?"

"A Wiccan priestess from Franklin," I point back with my thumb.

"You'd rather have a witch than your dad?"

"He told me he wouldn't do it."

"Stay right there."

Oh boy, we get to have a family argument again. I should get back in my car and leave. The way Dad comes outside, you'd think I exposed myself to Mom and asked her for directions to Albuquerque.

"Now, why are you trying to pit your mother against me?" Dad asks. "I raised you to respect boundaries, and you're crossing mine right now."

"No," I say. "Mom raised me. You threw a few Bible verses out around dinner time and expected me to be quiet around you."

"It's called respect," Dad says. "This new girl must have made you forget that."

"Okay," I say. "I hope you can live with yourself when your grandchild isn't in your life."

I turn to leave and he follows. I'm their only child, and he treats me like a step-son who is trying to break apart his marriage. All I wanted was for my parents to come to my ceremony.

"No parent is perfect," He calls after me, "But I never paid a bill late and you never missed a meal."

"There's more to being family than keeping someone alive," I get in the Volvo.

"You talking to me about love?" He asks. "Maybe if you'd come back to Jesus, you'd see I loved you more than anyone else ever could."

"What the fuck does even mean, Dad?"

"You curse at me and you've got the Devil's words coming straight from your lips."

Stepping out of the car, I look to see if any of the neighbors are watching from the street. No, I don't intend to hurt Dad. I came here hoping to speak rationally and he came out on offense mode.

"You don't accept me," I say. "I'm old enough to make my own decisions, and if you truly believed God had anything to do with my life, you'd let me go on my own path without your input. Once I moved out of your house and started paying my own bills, your opinion became null and void. I am a man, Dad. I'm taking care of my life like a man. I'm making sure if I have a child, they're kept alive like you did for me. In order to do that, I have to prioritize my happiness for a while. If you think I'm making a mistake, let me learn from it."

He turns away and goes back inside, so I leave too. Maybe Perry and Shannon will eventually accept me as their family, because mine seems to always run away from me. People may think my life is somehow perfect because of money and love, but I'm losing everyone I held dear.

Somer comes out of the bridal shop with a dress in a black bag she has to hold above her head. I didn't think she's get one today. Her face reminds me that there's joy in my world that I continue to reap the rewards from. When she kisses me and hugs me so tight that my ribs hurt, I can't hold onto any animosity I carried over from Dad.

"The lady who helped me suggested going to Belk for a suit," She says. "How'd it go with your parents?"

"They're not coming," I say.

"That'll be alright, sweetie," She pinches my cheek. "I'll dress Stevie up to look like your mama."

## Chapter 26

I am a millionaire, and money buys freedom. People believe they are free because they have the choice to either get in line or go off on their own. Either they wear the mask or they say the virus doesn't matter, it's not real, so why follow what the government says when they've been against us all along. As if wearing a garment over your nose and mouth is somehow stripping away your freedom. But the ones wearing the mask are supporting the liberal agenda; whatever that means. It's that kind of freedom that makes the world a giant petri dish for bacteria and disease. People are so obsessed with their freedom that they fail to realize they can't actually do whatever they want with their lives unless they have money.

But all of my money can't bribe my parents, use a church for a wedding ceremony, or convince anyone other than Somer's family to attend. I like that kind of equalization. People spend too much of their money and time on wedding ceremonies. I had a cousin get married in the town's largest Methodist church with everyone and his redneck brother in attendance, and the open bar, food, music, and honeymoon costed my aunt and uncle a year's salary at any cubicle job. That means, I would've worked at EHR for a year, and all of my money would cover one day for two people who ended up getting divorced four years later.

All Mom could say was, "And Virginia spent all that money for that wedding" as if wealth could force two people to get along until they died. My parents got married in a church the size of their living room and it didn't cost them a penny, but they didn't have much of a honeymoon or reception either.

Lynn and I were young college kids who were ethically opposed to ceremony in general. We got married by the Baptist Center minister on campus. Lynn's dad took us all out to Olive Garden afterward.

Somer spends the night in her childhood bedroom, and I drive to her house alone around 11:30. I'm wearing a suit I have no intention of ever wearing again. Margaret's car is parked behind Somer's Jetta, so I assume her parents are vetting her before the ceremony.

Before I can open the back gate, Perry unlocks the latch and reveals his blue golf shirt and khaki combo. Luckily, we didn't hire a photographer to showcase this affair.

"Come on back here," Perry says.

"Good to see you," I say.

"The witch is inside with the ladies."

"Where's Stevie?" I ask.

"He's not coming. He'll probably watch from his bedroom window. I can't get that boy to do shit."

"Maybe I'll get to meet him when he graduates high school," I say.

"Way things are going, he'll probably have to do it over Zoom."

We sit at a distance from each other and wait for Margaret to make her appearance. Somer hasn't texted me since last night, so I assume we're not going to speak until our vows. If only I could hit pause on Perry and me talking until then.

"Somer told me your parents couldn't make it," Perry says. "I might have been mad enough to hit you when we met, but I can't hold anything against my baby to the point I'd miss her getting married."

"I appreciate that," I say.

"My dad missed my wedding too."

"Oh yeah?"

"He died when I was seventeen."

Margaret wears a white blouse that almost reaches her knees with black capris and ankle high work boots. A blue scarf with glittering moons gives her an oddly ordained appearance. Perry motions for us to stand as Shannon runs past me to her husband. I assume it's my turn to walk over to Margaret, but she holds up her hand.

"Wait," She says. "You will come to the bride. She will not come to you."

A white cloud of lace and cotton appears at the sliding glass door. Somer's smile is expecting as she steps to Margaret's side. She's like a present I get to unwrap later.

"Now come."

I face Somer and try to take in the scene. It feels like we're kids playing house. In the short time we've known each other, Somer and I haven't had a fight. There's no strife in our bond. It's going to happen. Most couples end up breaking up once and getting back together. We're too secure, so this whole event suggests a schism in reality.

Margaret looks at her watch for a moment and sets her left hand down as if the ritual is time sensitive.

"Wednesday," Margaret starts, "April fifteenth, twenty-twenty. The time is precisely noon. Under the overcast sky in Newnan, Georgia, we gather to celebrate the union of two young souls. Marriage is a serious contract; the oldest and most personal of deals. Whether united in God's name or otherwise, wed by man or woman, you cannot enter this lightly. Before we begin the exchange of vows, does anyone present know of any reason these two should not be wed?"

Somer looks over my shoulder at what I assume is Stevie looking out his window. Perry and Shannon hold hands as my former classmate rubs a tissue against her tear duct.

"As stated, the groom must come to the bride first," Margaret says. "Wayne Pallidus, please repeat the following vows. I, Wayne..."

"I, Wayne... Swear my allegiance to my betrothed, Somer. My life is dedicated to her happiness, health, and prosperity. In illness or near demise, I will sacrifice myself for her survival. For me, marriage is forever... and I will uphold this promise... or may God or whichever entity I believe in strike me down if I violate our vows."

I wish we'd gone over these vows beforehand. That last line makes me think I'm already violating a previous contract.

"I, Somer... Accept Wayne's offering to my spirit and the responsibility for tending to his soul. If I so choose, I also accept his last name as mine as this is a gift signifying our union. While I shall keep his heart in the vice of my love forever, I pray that God or whoever I may or may not pray to shall guide us into eternity side by side."

Her vows are almost kinky, and I can't help but wonder if Margaret crafted them specifically for the women she marries.

"Somer," Margaret says, "Do you accept this man as your husband?"

"I do."

"Wayne, do you accept the terms of your union?"

"I do."

"If the bride consents, you may now kiss."

As soon as Somer runs to her parents, I pull out five one-hundred dollar bills and give them to Margaret. Without a word, she leaves through the gate. Given the nature of this ceremony, I'm not sure if I can get into Heaven if I just sold my soul to Somer.

Somer returns to me with her mother's tears on her, which I help her brush away.

"Let me go in and take this off," Somer says. "Mama wants to keep it on my old bed."

"Wayne!" Shannon runs over.

"Shannon," I say. "Did you do the reading for Thursday's class?"

"Oh, do you remember having to read *Orlando Furioso*?"

"Unfortunately, yet I remember nothing about it."

"Neither do I, but I can't remember most of what we read. I'm so happy you're part of my family now."

She hugs me as Perry walks into the house. Somer has to come with me to the new Newnan courthouse to get our papers officiated. There's a clause that asks whether or not we're blood related. What happens if you check Yes?

## Chapter 27

In the interest of seeing major cities and niche towns while most people are still at home, our first destination is Nashville, which is a little over four hours away. Rather than go back to the house after getting our marriage license officiated, I had our packed bags in the car during the ceremony. As I'm pulling onto I-85, Somer pulls out her phone to make a TikTok. Apparently, my first video received ten-thousand views.

"How does it feel to be married?" Somer asks.

"I have to remind myself every five seconds because there's no way I convinced you to marry me," I say.

"Oh, I would've said Yes if you'd asked me when we met," She pinches my cheek.

I-85 is a circuit powered by inconsiderate Yankees who ride your ass and cut you off, and the people from Alabama and Florida drive slower than an eighty-eight year old man's urine stream. We eased off each other the past few days, so my waterworks are recuperating. Luckily, Somer starts playing some band called Cocteau Twins, and my silence doesn't sound so loud.

With all the shadows looming over me, it's hard to pay attention to the light that's leading me. Each success is merely a pause before another failure in my experience. I had this same optimistic, happy feeling when I married Lynn. I thought that would be my forever. Did that marriage really end because of how my skin changed or how I failed to change with my wife?

I have to start thinking of Somer as my wife and Lynn as the past. Spent so much time thinking of both of them, I haven't given myself much thought. My dick and heart led me along this time.

One of the last days I remember before this change, I was standing in the bathroom at EHR Interactive with Wilson, and the realization that I was slowly losing my hair reminded me of my mortality. Some men lose their hair before they're even twenty-five. Others go gray early. My grandfather, Mom's daddy Thomas, didn't go bald or gray. Dad retains his color through boxed dye, but he didn't lose hair.

When you're twenty-eight, the clock doesn't slow down, and you're just now getting a chance to consider that age cannot evade anyone who doesn't die young. No one is twenty-nine. They're almost thirty. Then when we hit the third decade of our existence, the world stops caring as much. The news doesn't seem as sad if you get hit by a bus or drink yourself to death. People stop saying, "Oh, he was so young."

It's charming when you're in college and obsessed with death. Comes with being young and existential. But the late twenties are when you should've started living and started to think about the future.

I wasn't even able to support my little family a few months ago. Adulthood is supposed to be when you take care of yourself. Manhood is when you're ready to take care of the people you love. I haven't been able to really take care of me, though.

My dream was to write in the most insignificant genre that wouldn't bring me any notoriety. I couldn't be Batman, but I wanted to write him. Adults tell kids they can be whatever they want, and every man hanging on the back of a garbage truck to collect waste had a dream they didn't get to realize. People pity them, yet we could all end up worse off than making good money and breathing fresh air.

"What you studying?" Somer asks.

"Me," I say.

"Well, I was thinking about that hotel room," Somer says. "I haven't ever stayed in a room without my Mama and Daddy."

"Must be exciting," I say.

"Ain't you excited?" She asks. "All the things we're going to do to each other? We can get some Little Debbies on the way up too."

"You taste sweet enough to me."

"What does my butt taste like?"

"It's kinda salty."

Instead of stripping and messing up the sheets, I drop on the king sized bed face down and inhale the fibers on the duvet. Somer pulls me up to lie on her chest. Do we belong to each other? Can I call her my own? Does this mean to her what it should mean to me?

"Wayne," Somer says, "I'm scared."

"Why?"

"We're gonna have a baby."

"I know. I'd be scared too if I had someone growing in me waiting to come out."

"I'm still a baby, though."

"I'll take care of you too."

"But I'm gonna swell up like a bear gorging for hibernation. You're not going to love me anymore."

"Sure I will," I say. "I'll have more to nibble on when I work my way down to your thighs."

"You won't fuck me when I'm showing."

"I will if you let me," I say. "Sex is like riding a bicycle. It'll be nice to make it more like riding a four wheeler."

"Oh, baby, you got a way with words," Somer pulls on my ear.

"Do you really think I'll stop loving you?" I ask. "I worry you'll finally see that I'm the same color as algae."

"All the comments on TikTok are wondering how you got married," Somer says. "To me, I've never wanted someone more than you. I don't see how anyone couldn't want you too."

"I'd be the dumbest ass in the world to not love you."

I have to take a shower before we can eat the Zebra Cakes we bought at a CVS. Somer watches TV with a towel still between her legs when I come out. She lets me use her thigh as a pillow.

"I've been good up 'til now," Somer says. "We haven't watched any horror movies since we been together."

"I usually have a marathon in October," I say. "We can watch whatever you want."

"And I wanna go to the beach."

"We can detour to the coast on our way up," I say. "Book us a hotel near the ocean."

"Are you ever going to say No to me?"

"Nah," I say.

"We have to do a TikTok with you walking down Broadway tomorrow. Then we'll do one on the beach."

"I'll do you on the beach."

Unlike Nashville when I was able to lie down in the street for a video, Myrtle Beach looks as if COVID-19 never existed. As we sit against the hood of our car to look at the ocean, there're people without masks practically shoulder-to-shoulder walking in the sand. Having driven all this way to get here, I hate to tell Somer we shouldn't go out there. The novelty of having an empty beach, even for a few minutes, is what we talked about as we left Tennessee this morning.

"I bet there's less people on Emerald Isle," Somer says.

"Where's that?" I ask.

"North Carolina. David Sedaris has a beach house there."

"Do you think he'd let us stay at his place?"

"You don't know who David Sedaris is?" Somer asks.

"Is he the lead singer for Led Zeppelin or something?"

Before we get back in the car, Somer has me stand at the edge of this embankment overlooking the beach so we can document the reason why we're leaving almost as soon as we arrived. Apparently, we can Air BnB a beach house with a pool on Emerald Isle and stay right next to the sand. Why we didn't think this far ahead last night is beyond me. Impulsivity was supposed to drive this honeymoon, but we can still be random explorers while booking places to sleep, I suppose.

I'm not sure how the world became so divided, especially regarding the safety of others. Perhaps turning a blind eye to the bombings, drone attacks, and invasions doesn't only pertain to overseas, and we're willing to risk sacrificing other peoples' lives for our own amusement. When I was let go from work, my colleagues acted like I was a germ ready to permeate throughout the building. How many of them are on a beach ignoring all the warnings now?

Somer shows me comments on TikTok of people with random avatars telling others they're stupid sheep for wearing masks. I wonder if the world found out we could eradicate most viral diseases in a month's time if we'd all stay home and wear face coverings when we had to leave would anyone bother?

I can't hate people for being stupid, though. Then I'd be no different than the people who avoid me in public. Admittedly, I kind of want to go home and sleep in my own bed with Somer rather than roam the country. The nation isn't in a state of despair. It's a microbiological culture growing to ensure everyone suffers.

"What do you want, Wayne?" Somer asks.

We're leaving Myrtle Beach and I'm trying to pay attention to the GPS on how to drive the two hours to Emerald Isle. By the time we get there, we'll have to get McDonalds and watch Netflix before going to bed.

"I think this idea was better in spirit than in practice," I say.

"Why don't we spend a few days at this beach house." Somer says, "We'll Instacart some stuff to eat, I'll get a tan, we're fuck a lot, and we'll go home when we're sick of it."

"Yeah," I say. "I think I made the right decision in marrying you."

Oddly enough, the first fast food place that's open in Emerald Isle is a Dairy Queen, so we get four bacon cheeseburgers and two medium Oreo and M&M Blizzards to split. By the time we get to the house, we have to start eating the ice cream so it doesn't turn into goo. Their ice cream is basically frozen skim milk with sugar.

Unsurprisingly, the interior of the beach house is light green and blue walls with a ceiling fan in every room, a wicker glass top coffee table sits in the middle of overstuffed furniture, a fifty-inch TV is downstairs while an old CRT is in the bedroom, and there are photographs of the ocean framed on canvas when the beach is literally right outside. Admittedly, the master bedroom suite has a great view with a sliding glass door that leads to a rustic deck. The wallpaper in the bathroom with its pink flamingos and surfboards looks like something my grandmother would've picked out in 1982. As promised, there's a small pool on the way to the water, though surprisingly no hot tub. Who doesn't like cooking themselves in a nasty bubbling stew?

We end up eating our burgers outside while the little bit of light leaves the horizon. Somer plays music on her iPhone as a mood setter, though I don't recognize the song.

"Now that we're married," I say, "Do you have any regrets?"

"About marrying you? No. I feel like a destitute Victorian woman who got to marry the king."

"It does feel like I won a prize for a contest I never entered," I say.

"Well, you didn't mean to enter," Somer says. "God submitted for you."

She points at my wrist and in the dim lighting I see the skin that looks like it belongs to a lizard.

"If you hadn't changed, we wouldn't be here," She says. "And now we have more than just each other's company to look forward to."

"Are you ready for this?" I ask. "I still feel so young like I shouldn't be having a baby."

"Oh, I wish it could happen tomorrow," Somer says. "The way you are with me; how you treat me. This baby is gonna get spoiled."

# Chapter 28

Society seemingly reverted to the old ways before my time. I'm in a waiting room distanced from other men wearing masks as their wives give birth and recover from their bodies being used as baby cannons. Somer is getting a C-section, so I get a new scar to kiss around, and she doesn't have to risk damaging her clitoris or ripping her skin right down to her asshole. Plus, she gets the fun drugs.

I'm not allowed to see the baby until all the staff clear the room either. There are people dying here. The hospital has tents set up in the parking lot with patient beds and ventilators. Of course, as many idiots as possible are crowding stores for Christmas without masks while their grandmother and uncle are struggling to breathe. Nevermind the men in here who can't be with the mothers of their children, I suppose.

"I bet a lot of people are going to lose a bet when your baby comes out," A man says.

"Hmm?" I ask.

"Your baby might come out green," He says.

"Why would people bet on that?" I ask.

I know the answer, because I'm curious as well. I doubt my daughter is going to be green. There's something problematic about worrying about her skin color to begin with. Why would I care? As long as the baby isn't blue or purple, we're fine.

"At least he'd know it's his baby," Another man says.

"Pssh," He says. "Damn, you're right about that one."

A nurse enters the room and calls my name, so I get up to follow her to the room. All the equipment is gone, and Somer is asleep with her neck tilted to the left. No one bothered to lower the bed.

Another nurse is putting a clean wrapping around our daughter, Ayvah. We decided on a name that was both antiquated and commonly misspelled thanks to two additional letters. However, it seemed playground bully proof.

I'm seeing this bundle of skin with a nose for the first time. Most babies aren't cute when they're newborns. However, the nurse who hands her to me smiles as if we gave birth to the most beautiful baby she's ever seen. I sit in a chair next to Somer as she begins to snore.

Our parents aren't here to declare who Ayvah looks like, and I hope she favors Somer. Considering we've been together for almost a year and now have a baby, maybe she'll finally let me see her ugly side where she snaps over an insignificant problem and slams doors to signify that's pissed. So far, she's still a sweet woman who likes being around me.

As I'm looking at Ayvah, tears blur my vision as I can't get over how I'm holding the little person we made. This beats meeting Batman or Superman in real life. Jesus could come through the door and announce he forgives me for doubting his existence, and I wouldn't quit looking at this child.

"No fair," Somer croaks. "I haven't gotten to hold her."

"They didn't let you see her after you had her?" I ask.

"They sewed me up and I fell asleep. You should take your shirt off for skin to skin contact."

"I'll stay dressed for now," I say. "How do you feel?"

"I think I'll take a nap when we get home."

"Miss Ayvah is sleeping right now, so you already have a lot in common."

"I love napping," Somer says. "But who is Miss Ayvah?"

"Your baby," I say.

"Oh. I'm still a baby, though."

"So, I have two babies now."

When we leave the building and Somer is holding Ayvah in her wheelchair, I pull the car around as if we're stealing precious gems. We're taking this baby with us and no one is stopping to ask where we found her. It's our baby. However, the same excitement I felt when Somer moved in with me returns as if we're changing our lives for better or worse, and there's no predicting the outcome.

Somer looks like I brought home pizza and cheeseburgers when I take Ayvah out of the car. I tell her to let me bring the baby inside so I can help her walk, but she insists on following me. We put the baby's car seat on the floor in front of the couch and watch as if there's a puppy playing with a bone.

"Every muscle in my body feels like I've been asleep for ten years," Somer says. "But I don't want to ever take my eyes off her."

"Remember that nap you wanted to take?" I ask.

"Don't talk dirty in front of the baby," Somer says.

She lies back on the couch and puts her feet in my lap. Ayvah hasn't cried since I've been around her. Somer says she was squalling when she was born, but I haven't even heard so much as a coo from her. Mom claims when I was born, I didn't cry at all. I looked around the room trying to find answers.

This little girl isn't going to experience life the way I did. There're so many advantages given the access to technology and communication, but I was the last generation to experience a childhood before the internet pervaded everything. AOL was a novelty, and Dad didn't allow us to have internet in the house until I was almost in junior high because he needed to run the church's website and email. I had to experience the online world when I was permitted at school. By the time I was in high school, students needed a computer for homework, but I had to do everything on the desktop PC Dad used. Kids have tablets today they can use for almost anything digital, and I had a Gameboy Color with only Mario and Pokemon. Ayvah won't know what it's like to have a toy box in the living room to keep her occupied while we watch something she considers boring. I could put the kibosh on letting her have whatever gadget will be in vogue when she's old enough to start pointing at the TV and asking for stuff, but eventually every parent has to relent some.

I wonder what the world will feel like to her as she grows. How would I turn out if I was born in the middle of a pandemic? Add in a father with green skin, and there's no telling how she'll perceive the world. Especially if I can keep Dad out of this.

Neither of my parents reached out after the ceremony. Instead, I had to read an interview with Dad in the Atlanta Journal when Steve Sebastian got in touch with him. Without any regard for how people perceive either of us, he said my affliction was the result of my sin and he could no longer help me as I was getting remarried too early and no longer respected him.

As much as I love Mom, she's letting Dad come between all of us. As his wife, she could step up and tell him to stop treating me like a Judas. Neither of them met my wife, the mother of their granddaughter, which is the greater sin in my mind. I suppose the positive side is that Perry and Shannon aren't religious, so they won't try entrenching any beliefs into Ayvah we don't want.

Still, I can't help wondering if Dad will break when his curiosity of his grandchild takes over. Once Somer is asleep, I take Ayvah to her room across from ours and sit on the floor with my phone dialing him.

"Well," He answers, "Been about nine months since I last talked to you, so I reckon your woman had her baby."

"Yes, Somer, my wife, had Ayvah," I say. "You're a grandfather now."

"You named a baby after Ava Gardner?"

"It's not spelled that way, but close. Are you going to tell Steve Sebastian all about it?"

"I made a deal with him," Dad says.

"Of course you did."

"Now, you don't know what deal I made."

"Enlighten me, Dad."

"I said I'd give him his interview if he'd stop bothering us. All of us."

"That might work, but he did lie to me about having Lynn in that documentary."

"He mentioned you fired a gun in his general direction, and I informed him I owned the same gun, but I'd never aim it anywhere I couldn't hit a man who came on my property."

"Doesn't God consider murder a sin?" I ask.

"I didn't say I'd murder nobody."

"Do you want to see Ayvah?" I ask.

"I been preaching every Sunday, and you know West Georgia has classes on campus again. If I catch the COVID, I don't want to give it to y'all."

"Yeah, okay."

"You gonna get the vaccination?"

"Sure," I say. "I'll get all the shots they want to give me."

"They can use me as a guinea pig."

Somer usually ends up waking up to take care of Ayvah at night because she usually wants milk. Unfortunately, I can't produce it. If she needs changing, Somer shakes me and I help with that. Seems like a fair trade, and I keep the baby in the living room during the day when Somer naps to make up for the lost sleep.

But today when my daughter starts crying, she doesn't need a change, and she won't take a bottle. I try singing to her outside, yet Ayvah keeps going. So, I decide to take her on a drive. If Somer wakes up, she can call me.

There's one song that I remember my parents singing and dancing to, and it wasn't often, but I try remembering the words because I sure as hell don't remember the singer. I type "sweet lord" in Spotify. Some guy named George Harrison pops up.

The acoustic guitar silences Ayvah. I drive the road I know. After the song plays a few times, I am almost in Whitesburg.

I like the idea of God, but not the harsh one Dad preaches about. So many Christians talk about Jesus and God being one and the same, yet Jesus speaks about love. Those who violate the many laws found in the Old Testament do not qualify for the eternal forgiveness and love found in the New Testament according to the men and women who use that book to control people. George Harrison's refrain is my take. If God is Love, then God cannot hate anyone. He accepts us because He made all of us who we are through the seed we grow from. That kind of love doesn't cease even for the miserable.

Despite not paying attention to news, I found out about Wilson, Lisa, Kendra, and everyone I used to work with getting laid off from EHR Interactive on Reddit. As predicted, their jobs were outsourced to the India branch. The building that I worked in is now empty. None of the lights are on inside. A large For Sale sign sits in the garden next to the dried up fountain.

I check on Ayvah in the back, and she's looking back at me in silence. I pull her out of her seat to show her the beast that nearly took her father's entire life. If I hadn't turned green, I would've been like everyone else in here. Sent home with the hope that the cost of having everyone work remote would let us keep our jobs only to see the company that employed so many hopeful college grads and people in their forties and fifties tired of working on their feet implode. The awards and software the higher ups boasted about for years amounted to a lot of wasted time.

A car pulls into the parking lot. I look around expecting to see security or someone wanting to talk to the green man. Instead, there's the Versa. Lynn and I rode all over the state, through Alabama, and to Florida in that car. I figured once the lease on our apartment was up in April, she'd move. Maybe she was feeling nostalgic too.

"Who let you have a baby?" Lynn rolls down her window.

"It grew from a tumor on my back," I say.

"Thought you were in Newnan these days?"

"I took Ayvah on a drive to help her get to sleep."

Lynn gets out and I let her take Ayvah into her arms. I'm surprised at my lack of hesitation, but also how willingly she holds the baby. We were supposed to do this together. Our baby would've been over a year old, I think.

"She's so tiny," Lynn says.

"I guess that's one thing she got from me," I say.

"Your nose too. That's what I first noticed about you."

"My nose?" I ask. "And I thought you didn't remember when we first met?"

"Well, you know I hate my nose, so I thought if we ever had a baby, it might have your nose instead."

Ayvah sighs and stretches, and I see Lynn smile for the first time in over a year. What could I have done to make her happy even for a moment? I suppose I technically did since I helped make my daughter. Everyone who smiles at her is appreciating my greatest achievement.

"You still live at the apartment?" I ask.

"Yeah," Lynn says. "I have a new roommate."

She hands my daughter back to me and turns back to the Versa.

"I gotta go."

"Are you feeling better?" I ask.

"Sure," Lynn says. "I guess I'm in a better place."

"That makes me happy," I say. "I hoped you'd get through it."

Without acknowledging what I say, Lynn shuts her door and gives a wave before driving out of the parking lot. She didn't even put her seatbelt on.

During the ride back to the house, I think about my old life. There's a possibility I'll step back into my parents' home, go into my childhood bedroom, taste Mom's chili, and see them dance to "My Sweet Lord" again. I don't mourn what I can go back to. While I saw the empty office building, I couldn't swipe my badge to go back inside. My cubicle isn't there anymore. Similarly, the woman I loved, who I exchanged vows with, and saw in the flesh once again will never let me back into her life, and I don't want to go back.

My new future sleeps in the backseat while my present waits for me at home. That's what I look forward to, and all I have to do is wait.

Made in the USA
Coppell, TX
08 March 2023